RISE OF THE
GREY PRINCE

I0631528

Praise for *'The Saga of Agni'*

'Intrigued by Indian myths, fairy tales and legends Arka Chakrabarti has penned a book full of mystical twists.'

— The Asian Age.

'Holding a maze of mystical twists and turns, the book builds up a crescendo of suspense, finally culminating into a gripping climax.'

— Deccan Chronicles.

RISE OF THE GREY PRINCE

THE SAGA OF AGNI

Arka Chakrabarti

Srishti
PUBLISHERS & DISTRIBUTORS

SRISHTI PUBLISHERS & DISTRIBUTORS
N-16, C. R. Park
New Delhi 110 019
editorial@srishtipublishers.com

First published by
Srishti Publishers & Distributors in 2015

10 9 8 7 6 5 4 3 2 1

It is said that there are moments in a man's life — neither many nor sparse, but quite a few of them — which leave an eternal mark on his life. He knows those imprints are not only his, but will be there even after he is long gone. I have experienced one such moment until today, that which is inexplicable amidst the extraordinary — it is that day when I saw her face for the first time, my beautiful angel, my daughter Annapurna Chakrabarti.

I dedicate this novel to her. What is one novel when I will be upholding the lifelong dedication of a father, rather happily!

Acknowledgements

I remember the day I had completed the first novel in the series 'The Saga of Agni', *The Secrets of the Dark*. It was a beautiful day; 'beautiful' is an understatement, for the word I seek is marvellous. I was barely twenty-four and it was just a copy, a simple-looking copy with many words scribbled inside it. Neither pretty to look at, nor clean at the edges; but a thing of utmost happiness and a beauty to my eyes.

I never thought it would take the form of an actual book, let alone a saga. I remember reading it to my good friends at first. Then I read it to my mother, the most inspiring figure in my life, then my father, then to my wife, then to my sister and so on. You can neither find more patient listeners than these, nor more inspiring ones. They dared to dream for me the dreams which I never dared myself. I just wanted everyone to know of the world of Gaya, but then a miracle happened. I got an email from Srishti Publishers & Distributors, wanting to read my work. The story after that is for you all to hold in your hands. I shall stay forever indebted to Srishti, not to forget the fellow dreamers who always walk beside me. I simply shudder in excitement to think that one day my daughter will grow up and read a book written by her father.

I again thank my father Tarun Kumar Chakrabarti; my mother Sukanya Chakrabarti; my wife Tultul Chakrabarti; my angel Annapurna Chakrabarti for coming to us; my greatest critic and best of friends – my elder sister Anindita Chakrabarti and my brother-in-law Arambhik Ghosh; and last but not the least, my wonderful companions, my friends.

Also, I thank all of you who have been kind enough to read my work and show your valuable appreciation – those who have taken out the time to send me the emails with such inspiring words and those who still inquire of when the second part is coming out. Your enthusiasm is the force that drives me. I remember not picking up the pen intentionally at times, and then getting your mails that broke the deadlock in my heart. I thank you again with all my heart, because you have shown me that Gaya belongs to us all.

Let the journey begin…

The Scroll

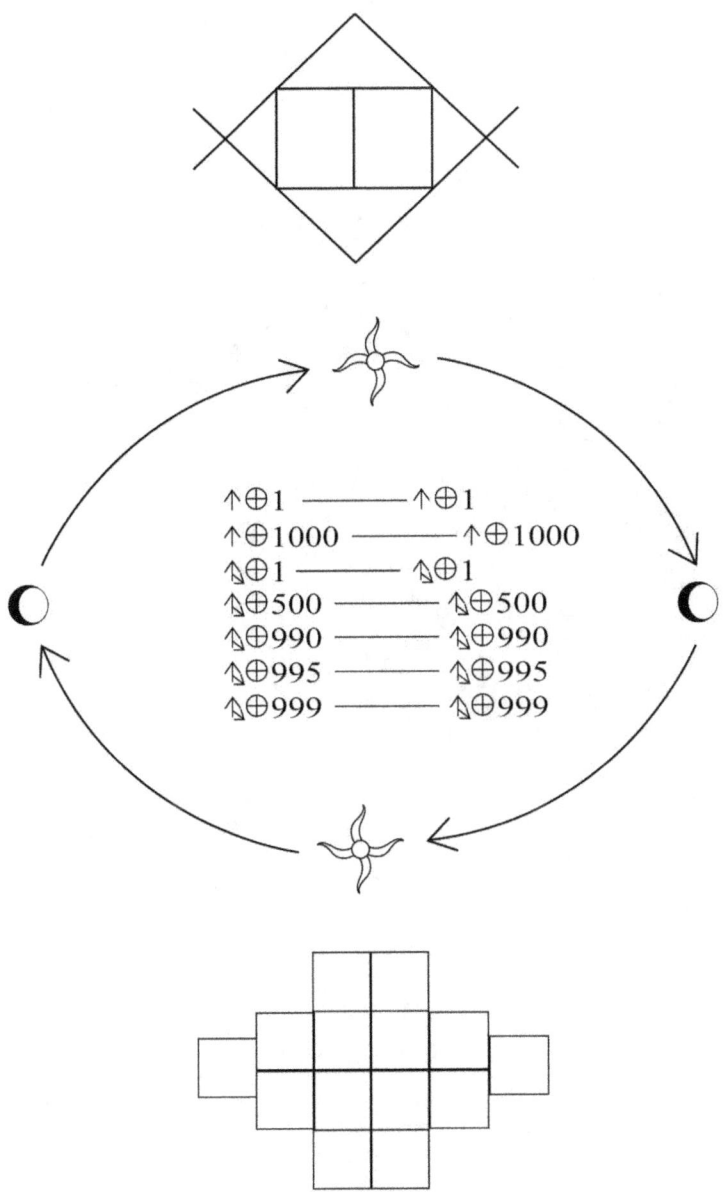

Map of Gaya

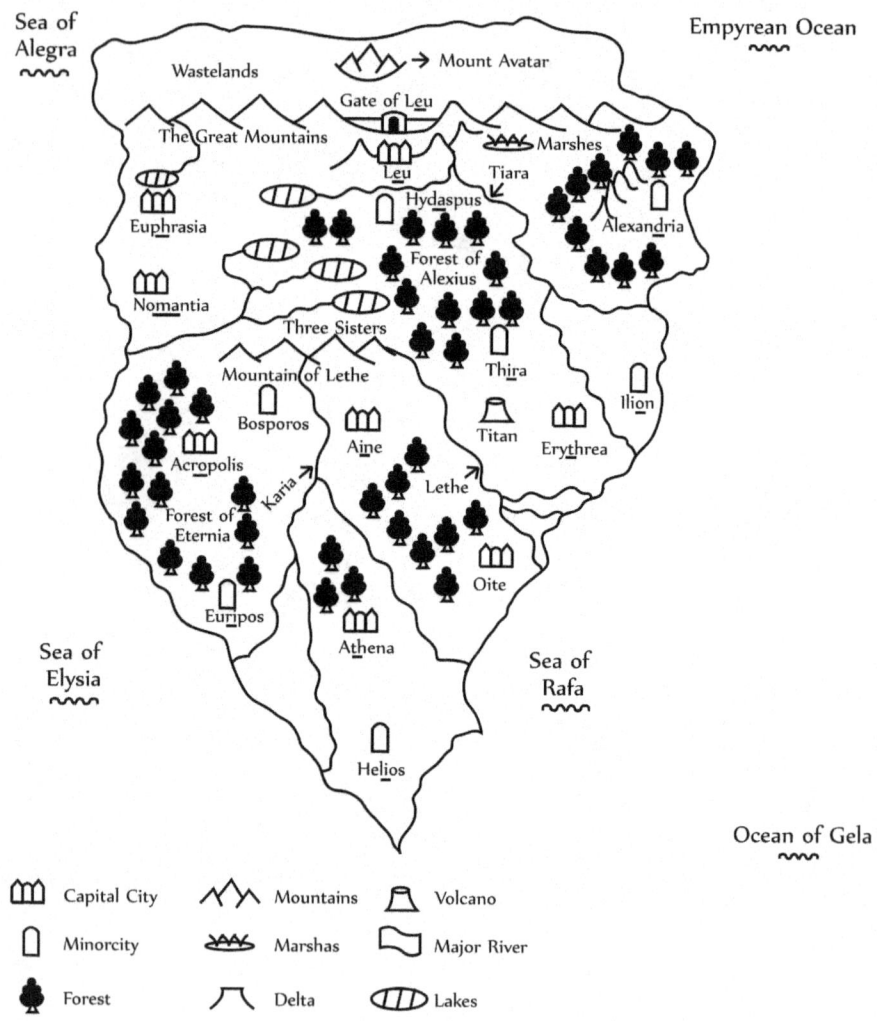

Sea of Alegra

Empyrean Ocean

Wastelands

→ Mount Avatar

Gate of Leu

The Great Mountains

Marshes

Leu

Tiara

Euphrasia

Hydaspus

Alexandria

Forest of Alexius

Nomantia

Three Sisters

Mountain of Lethe

Thira

Ilion

Bosporos

Aine

Titan

Erythrea

Acropolis

Karia

Lethe

Forest of Eternia

Oite

Euripos

Athena

Sea of Elysia

Sea of Rafa

Helios

Ocean of Gela

	Capital City		Mountains		Volcano
	Minorcity		Marshas		Major River
	Forest		Delta		Lakes

Map of Gaya

The story so far

Gaya is a land of mystery and magic, divided into two continents – The Land of the Rising Sun and The Land of the Setting Sun. While the former is a cluster of many kingdoms, the latter is under the thumb of The Abode of the Seven. The Abode is also the upholder of the twin prophecies of sage Darshana that speak of the end of Gaya at the hands of the destroyer – he who shall be born of the royal seed in 'The Land of the Setting Sun'. Thus, under the decree of the Seven Guardians of the 'The Abode', no prince is allowed to live for the fear of the emergence of the destroyer, the wielder of the black flames.

But a king, a father, defies the will of the Seven and smuggles the prince of the continent at the expense of his life. Agni, unaware of his past, grows up as the ward of Raja Adhirath of Himadri alongside Prince Yani and his trusted friend Vrish, the son of Briksha, the man who had played a pivotal role in Agni's escape. Briksha's son Vrish and daughter Malini – whom Agni is engaged to marry – are the closest to what Agni calls family.

A fire during the festival of Trinetra consumes everyone who Agni so dearly loves, barring Vrish. All he can find is Malini's charred body while she is breathing her last. Her throat slit and left to burn, she gives him a clue that could eventually lead to the one responsible for the fire, her killer. The clue is a symbol, ancient and unknown. Thus begins Agni's race against time to hunt down the perpetrator.

On the other hand, 'The Land of the Setting Sun' is war-torn. Warrior Princess Lysandra prepares to lead the Army of Leu against the tyranny of 'The Abode'. The war for the reclamation of Alexandria which had been turned to ashes by the Seven leads the famed warrior princess to face the fourth of the Seven Guardians, The Beast. The princess's army tastes victory, but at the expense of a mystery – the reason behind such indomitable might of the Seven Guardians.

Back in 'The Land of the Rising Sun', Agni chases the culprit to Nisarga, ultimately tracking him down with the help of Prince Yani, Vrish and Sir Lonan, the ambassador from the West. Sir Lonan, who poses as Sir Drake to win Agni's confidence in Himadri reveals his true intent in bringing Agni in front of the Seven. The stranger behind the fire that burnt Agni's family had been wounded by Sir Lonan's poisoned dagger in the final skirmish before his death. But he reveals on his deathbed that he was Agni's ally, protecting him and his identity. Since Malini had overheard their conversation and had become aware of Briksha's identity, he had no choice but to kill them all to protect the secret of Agni's heritage. The final revelation – 'the twin prophecies' for which Agni is being hunted, are not the entire truth, for there is a third prophecy which Agni's father King Arkansas knew, which had remained hidden for ages in Nisarga – turns the tables again. The Abode never wanted it found and so it has been kept a secret ever since. Agni finds the third prophecy, only to find a long forgotten riddle from the ancient lore of Gaya. It is for Agni to uncover the third prophecy and find the truth.

Prologue

The sky was dark, but beams of moonlight bathed the towers of Athena. Then came a swarm of clouds, bringing along the darkest hours. The lanterns of the deserted corridors dimmed in the last few drops of oil. The first turn of the night watchmen was drawing to an end.

The deserted hallways were swept by the gusts of bitter cold wind and the window shutters continued to rattle.

'The dawn shall come with a new age at its door,
A legend will be born from the ancient folklore.
But the morning will not be in the shade of gold,
A red dawn for man shall unfold.
He who shall walk as the son of a King,
Will see the fortitude of man and the blossoms of spring.
But as he shall step on the land forsaken,
His will shall be broken and his soul will be taken.
Gaya will weep and watch the final battle of mankind,
The Sun shall darken and 'The Maker' will be blind.
As the day will end, alone in the ashes will he stand,
The dark fire swirling around him in the barren wasteland.

All is foretold, for no man shall arise and be so bold,
To hinder the flow of time and the ways of old.'
                              - The voice of Darshana, 'The Steps to Destiny'

King Arkansas closed the book with a sad smile on his face.

"But why Arkansas?" came a voice from behind one of the closed doors of the palace of Athena. "If we walk this path, all our efforts shall be in vain."

"You are wrong there, my dear friend. It is not our choice. It was never to begin with. I understand that now, but the burden is too much to bear," replied the king.

"Then what will happen to your son? Solon cannot hide him for his entire life, and one day or the other they will find him. Then what will happen? History will repeat itself."

King Arkansas closed his eyes to the unbearable thought. "What other choice do I have? What if they succeed this time? After what I saw...," the king paused.

"How can I place a bet on my own son's life?" the voice faded.

"And what about the six before?" King Arkansas looked up.

"That was not in my power."

"Exactly. Now, it is in your hands. At least one can try," said the other man.

King Arkansas stood up.

"If it is their fate we have to decide then we shall leave it on them. For I have seen the way to which it all leads. Ketu was right all along, the burden is too much to bear and it is the chosen who shall decide on the fate of all."

"And can you trust your son to do all this? Can you trust your blood?"

The King simply smiled.

"It is true, he is yet to be born and still I am putting such a great burden on his shoulders even before he has set foot on mother Gaya, a child should not born with the tide of times nestling on its shoulders, it is cruel even for 'The maker', I can only pray."

The man drew his hood down.

"Then we don't have much time. The sands of time flows, the hour draws near and again we leave everything to fate. I hope he grows strong enough in our absence to carry such a burden for it is truly cruel and unwise."

"May be that was our choice all along," the soft smile on the King's face was full of grief and sadness.

The Gnawing Darkness
(The Land of the Setting Sun)

"A blessed morning to you, good sir! Can I interest you in buying some spiced wine?"

The passerby stopped and said gruffly, "And how are you, an outsider, selling it here? Have you taken permission from the elder?"

"You must be mistaken, my good man. My name is Charis, the son of Sleven, and I have been selling here for the past ten years. I was born here and I took over my father's business when I was barely eighteen suns old." That's when the trader grew suspicious and asked, "But I have never seen you around. Who are you? And do you live here, by the way?" The smirk was clear on his face.

The man caught the trader by his collar and shouted, "Sleven's son died seven years back and Sleven is a good friend of mine. Don't know who you are lad, but better get lost before I kick you head out."

"What's happening there, Boris? Is everything alright?" Fear crept into Charis's eyes as two more men came and stood beside the man who had been questioning him.

"This lad says that he is the son of Sleven, back from the dead," mocked the middle-aged man.

"Then let us send this liar back to where he came from," said another.

Charis was sweating. "You are mistaken. I am Charis and my wife's name is Sharia. We have two children and we have been living here for the past twenty years."

Boris slapped him hard across the face and spat, "Sharia is my daughter and she has mothered two children with Garreth, my son-in-law. I will skin you alive if you slander her name, you imposter."

Charis broke free from the man's grasp and started running. He ran as fast as his legs would carry and he did not look back.

"Come back you bastard," the shouts were thinning.

He ran and ran, crossed the wheat fields, and then fell on the mud road. He could see his house, the very place where his beloved Sharia would be waiting for him with their two little angels. The sweat was wisped away from his brows by the cool wind and he could hardly wait to get into his house. How glad was he to have escaped that mad man, that complete lunatic who said that his beloved Sharia was someone else's.

He spared a fleeting glance to the old lady cutting crops on the field adjacent to their house. Then he came to a sudden halt — his face contorted in fear, his breathing became heavy. *How can it be?*

In place of his house stood an old, charred building enveloped in wild shrubs. The climbers had gripped the moss covered walls and house stood gutted.

"Why do you always do this to yourself? It is time to let go, son," came the voice of the old lady from the adjacent field.

"Wh... What?" he asked bewildered.

"They are gone, lad. They have been gone for the past seven years. The fire took them and it was unfair. Sharia was a wonderful girl, but it has been too long, too long even to grieve anymore," said the old woman in her sympathy-laden voice.

"What are you saying?" he stuttered.

The old woman shook her head, slowly rising to reach out to him. She came and placed a hand of compassion on his shoulders. "You lost your family, and it must be hard. But it's time you let go."

"Seven years? What in the name of the maker are you saying? I saw them here this very morning."

▼

The Lord of Light slowly took his hand away from the man kneeling in front of him. He was drooling and bore a blank look on his face.

The man stood up slowly and looked around. Some of the houses of the village were burnt down, while some still stood. There were corpses everywhere. A few that were alive had turned into something else: they walked, they saw and they breathed, but that was all.

"What happened here?" asked Aqua slowly.

"He is up to his old games again," replied the Lord of Light.

"But why?"

Silence was the only answer. Just then came the voice of the light bringer, "My Lord!"

The Lord of Light turned to see his kneeling servant.

"My Lord, I think you should come and see this for yourself."

The Lord eyed the man with indifference and started walking towards the graveyard with Aqua right behind him. The servant scurried along.

"Forgive us, my Lord, but we did not know what to do."

Lord Light kept on gazing, the repulsion clear on his face. The graveyard was dug from inch to inch, only the tombstones remained. Nameless, as if something had etched back the stones to their original form and the names were never sculpted on them at all. The coffins were laid out in the open, but none of them had any corpses.

'All the coffins were empty, a graveyard of ghosts,' the servant whispered.

The frigid look on Lord of Light's face and the clenched jaw couldn't hide what his servants had failed to see — fear.

'He is becoming stronger. It has begun.'

The Calling of Fate
(The Land of the Setting Sun)

The great iron gate of Leu was thrown open. The tales of bravado of the Lions engraved on it shone brighter with the return of the heroes. Drums were beaten and flower petals showered like rain drops, bringing a smile on the weary faces of those being welcomed back home.

Lysandra led them to the stairs of the Senate where Agapito stood smiling. They were greeted with the formal salute of one hundred court guards.

"Disperse," shouted Torman and Lysandra came down from her horse. She paused for a moment and looked around at the weary lions embracing their loved ones. Her thoughts went back to her father. She walked up to the members of the Senate with a smile. They had gathered to welcome her home and congratulate her on her great feat.

"Our faith was not misplaced. Thus returns the lioness of Leu, victorious," greeted Agapito.

"We never doubted her for a single moment. She is her father's daughter after all," said another.

"I serve Leu," she replied humbly.

"The best than any woman can," said Agapito.

She smiled and whispered, "Uncle I have something to discuss with you."

Agapito gave her a searching look and then turned to the other senators, "My fellow senators, today is a wonderful day indeed and the words shall never stop flowing. But we must let our weary guardian take some well-deserved rest."

"Indeed. But we shall listen to your great tales of battle. There is no escape from that," said one of the younger Senators, the admiration clear on his face.

"Certainly," she replied with a smile.

"Off course and she will be happy to do so but now is the time to part ways," declared Agapito casting a glance at the young man.

The Senators gave their parting greetings and went their way. Agapito led Lysandra and Torman to their own quarters.

"You days of torment are just starting, for young men will plague you more than they ever did before," stated Agapito.

"And I shall deter them, as always...But how is father?" was her first question.

"He is fine; just a little .... you know him."

She smiled and Agapito asked her about Damian.

"The same since I sent you word," replied Lysandra.

Agapito gave a concerned nod, but then the smile came back to his face. "He is a strong man, young and agile. Take heart. I have called upon 'Zoe' of Nomantia, the best healer of the North and she is supposed to reach Leu by today. She always finds a cure."

"But she has strong ties with Lord Varca," spoke Torman with a questioning look on his face.

"Don't be alarmed General, Varca has not sided against us... not yet."

"But he will not side with us too," said Torman grimly.

"Maybe, maybe not. But why not wisp away their best healer for the time being," said Agapito smiling at Lysandra.

"I thank you uncle," she spoke from gratitude.

"Ahh, don't be silly! Damian is more than your brother you know. He is my nephew as well."

She was smiling at his words when he spoke again, "Now tell me of this urgent matter of yours which has stopped you from visiting your father?"

Lysandra stopped and asked, "Where is Demetrius now?"

"I do not know for certain, but he should be in his estate. He took a few days' leave from the Senate stating illness."

Lysandra was smiling at Torman, who himself had a faint smile on his face.

Agapito looked from Lysandra to Torman. "What is amiss?"

▼

Agapito sat still, his fingers clasped together, his eyes shut. "This is a very serious accusation, even for the likes of Demetrius."

He stood up and started for his study desk. "These are troubled times indeed. First the Seven, and now Demetrius."

While he poured some wine into two glasses, Torman spoke, "But we are not absolutely certain about this invulnerability of the Seven. The last I saw that thing was somewhere on the sea bed."

"Even so," said Agapito handing Torman a glass. "You and Lysandra had a hard time just dealing with one of them and that too with the help of that strange weapon. I simply shudder at the thought of facing the six of them together in a battlefield."

"We can handle them; leave the military matters to me."

"No one doubts your stance, Torman, but the Seven are no ordinary foes. I have heard of many tales of their strange power," Agapito sipped some wine.

"Tales can be misleading," declared Torman and did not touch his cup. Agapito shook his head.

"And what about Demetrius?" Lysandra changed the subject.

"A very complicated situation indeed! We can make a decisive move only once we have clear evidence."

"We have evidence against him," came Torman's voice. As Lysandra and Agapito looked at him, Torman continued, "His seal, I have seen his seal on that thing when we were inspecting it after the battle."

Agapito leaned back, and said after much thought, "If that is the case, then we must seal that object away. There couldn't be any more hard evidence."

Lysandra's face lit up. "That's excellent news. We can clear Leu of his filth once and for all."

"It's not that easy. Open courts tend to prolong judgement, and he being a member of the Senate, several other factors shall come into play," replied Agapito. "He can say that he was unaware of the object's true nature and then if the votes go in his favour, we won't have a choice but to grant him minor punishment for negligence."

"Negligence! Good soldiers lost their lives and so did innumerable innocent souls. How can it ever pass as mere negligence?" stormed Torman.

"Politics is a vile thing, my friend," shrugged Agapito.

Lysandra smile was lost as swiftly as it had appeared. And Agapito was yet again prompt to bring it back, "Anyhow, every man and woman deserves respite from their troubles; you being the most deserving now. Let us not ponder on these things for the moment, we have tomorrow. For now, your father is waiting for you."

Lysandra was waiting for Agapito to finish so that she could go and see her father. That's when he said dreamily, "All this talk about invulnerability brings back memories of that man."

Lysandra's curiosity was somewhat stirred, "Which man, uncle?"

"I forget his real name but we used to call him 'Sage'. He was quite the storyteller."

"Not again," said Torman disgusted. But Agapito paid him little heed. "You know of 'Nisarga'?" he asked Lysandra.

"Not much," she admitted, "Just that it's one of the greater cities of the East."

"Yes, and there is a story behind it from what Sage used to say. It is said the city of 'Nisarga' was first a great seat of learning founded by Darshana."

"Not those damned prophecies again," cut in Torman.

"Can you just wait and listen," replied an irritated Agapito, and continued to Lysandra, "Well, it is said that the city was built as a colony of Hala, but was later freed by a general to build Nisarga. But Sage used to say that it was not the entire truth. The vast armies of Hala could not have been defeated by the General's entire forces, but are said to have been defeated by a single man."

"A single man?" repeated Lysandra, just as amazed as curious.

"Yes," said Agapito, adding a bit of mystic, "A terrible being. Who could not be slain by swords or arrows. A man bred for war."

"How can you breed men for war?" asked Torman scornfully.

"It's just a tale Torman. Use your imagination!" replied Agapito.

Then he looked at Lysandra. "From then, The Land of the Rising Sun trembled with the mere mention of this being. They named him Asura, meaning demon."

"Folklore and fables, meaningless!" Torman stood up abruptly.

Agapito was not pleased. "It is just a story, Torman. It doesn't need to have a meaning. I scare my grandchildren to sleep with this tale."

"Then you must excuse me. I am too old for stories and too tired," replied Torman.

"Very well, let us meet tomorrow then when our spirits are restored and then we shall have more meaningful conversations."

Torman gave a nod and asked Lysandra, "Lys, you coming?" But she was lost in her own world.

"Lysandra," Agapito called out softly and she came to her senses.

"Yes General, I am," she replied quickly. "I thank you for your wonderful story, uncle."

"You are too kind," replied Agapito smiling.

They bid him goodbye and soon after Torman went his way, Lysandra was left to herself. The word 'asura' ringing in her ears.

▼

'Truth alone can justify the order of creation but knowledge within the reach of many shall lead to destruction. So the Seven of the Seven shall guard the realm of man, their comings and goings unknown.'

"There you are!" came Torman's voice which startled Lysandra.

"I have been looking for you everywhere," his loud voice echoed in the library. Then his eyes fell on the book in her hand.

"What are you doing here anyways?"

She closed the book. "I have been going through a few things. The Abode was founded some fifteen hundred years back. That's twenty five generations roughly. Yet we know nothing of them. Where do they come from and where do they go? Is it possible not to have any records for twenty five generations?"

"Not this again," replied Torman exasperated.

"But doesn't it surprise you?" she asked.

"They like to keep their order secret, like many," he replied glibly.

"Yes, but…" She stopped mid-sentence as Torman raised his hand.

"We can stand here and argue all day or…," he paused with a smile. The frown on Lysandra's face quickly metamorphosed into a smile as he completed, '…or you can come and see Damian."

She jumped up without a word. She let the wind carry her the distance and didn't even wait for Torman. She was just about to take the bend when she heard a woman's raised voice.

"I don't know when. And don't you think even if I had known, I wouldn't have said it out loud. He is young and should be able to resist more. It's the same disease."

Lysandra slowly took the turn and saw Agapito, on the verge of saying something. Just then he spotted Lysandra. "Ah, Lys! We have been waiting for you," he said quickly, with a made up smile.

Lysandra's eyes fell on the other figure: a short woman, grey and wrinkled with a crooked look, her eyes pale yellow. She was staring at her intently.

"How is Damian?" she asked looking at Agapito.

"He has just woken up, a bit fragile but he will recover."

"He needs rest," spoke the woman.

"Yes, yes! Lysandra, this is Zoe and Zoe, this is the pride of Leu, Princess Lysandra."

She gave a nod but Lysandra kept staring at her. It seemed to her that they had met before.

"Well Zoe, I am glad you two have met. I will walk you out," Agapito broke the silence and started walking.

The woman followed suit in silence. Agapito turned to look at Lysandra, "You go and meet Damian. I will be back soon."

Lysandra saw them disappear around the bend.

The first encounter
(The Land of the Setting Sun)

The river Lethe broke into three channels to the south of Erythrea forming the fertile delta of the Erythrean farmlands. It was also the nestling den of the Silk fish, a local delicacy. They had derived their name from the shining scales on them and their translucent fins. They swam upstream during monsoon to the breeding grounds.

It was a few bell hours past dawn. Two fishermen were rolling their nets, their fishing boat roped to the beach.

"It was a good morning," smiled one of them.

"Aye, a blessed morning indeed. I wonder how much this lot will fetch us?" said the other.

"A few nuggets for each at least."

The waves were crashing on the narrow stretch of the beach, the turbulent water swirled at the confluence of the river and the ocean.

"What is that?" asked one of them pointing at something in the water.

"Where?" asked the other, his hand shielding his eyes from the sun.

All colour vanished from their faces when they saw a man walk out from the water, slowly and started walking towards the tree line.

"Did you see that?" whispered one of the fishermen to another.

The man paused and turned his gaze towards the duo.

"You took your time," came a whisper from the shadows of the tree.

The man started walking again and entered the mangrove forest. A hooded figure stood there dressed in black.

"You are not needed here, Dark. I can find my own way back," said the man, the Beast.

"I thought I should come and welcome you back, after your grand victory," came the mocking reply.

"Don't you dare mock me," snarled the Beast.

"What else must I do? You were beaten by an old man and a girl. Maybe I should not have left you there all alone."

The Beast's eyes became red with rage, and he bared his fangs. "Not one more word."

Dark appeared in front of him, "Tame your anger, old friend! I am not your foe."

"Think before you mock me the next time; because I won't hesitate."

"I want you to see what you cannot. You are blinded by your rage," replied Dark.

The Beast looked away, his fists clenched. "I will rip them off to pieces. I will burn Leu to ashes."

"Can you?" asked Dark with a calmness rare for Beast.

The Beast's eyes looked furious when he said, "Yes I can, and I will. And if you do not stop mocking me, I will make sure that you suffer the same fate as them."

Dark broke into a laugh. The Beast could not hold himself back anymore and grabbed Dark by his throat. Dark dissipated in his hands and reappeared at a distance.

"Your strength is waning like before. History does repeat itself."

The Beast stood there silent, and. Dark walked closer to him.

"We need him and you know it. It must come to an end. We must become whole again," Dark's voice was more anxious than mocking.

"We have been looking for him for two decades now; all our attempts have failed," replied the Beast.

"That is why this time one of us has to go. The time draws near."

The Beast was staring at his black eyes. "What about Light?" he asked.

Dark smiled. "He doesn't have to know that you were even here."

"Very well, but if you betray me too..."

Dark slowly shook his head. "It won't come to that...And don't forget to take care of our guests on your way out."

The Beast grinned, "With pleasure." He turned his gaze towards the two fishermen hiding behind a tree trunk.

Dark slowly walked away. 'The time is near, it shall be fulfilled', he said to himself and heart-wrenching screams of two souls echoed in the forest.

▼

Damian had opened his eyes almost six weeks, albeit without any recollection of the events inside the ship after his capture. The strangest fact was that the Abode had sent an emissary for peace, allowing the Senate the right to choose their king. Demetrius was yet to be found and his absence mixed with controversies of his betrayal was slowly turning things in their favour. Most believed he had left Leu after the Abode's army was routed.

The winter showers had started and it washed away the taint from the land. The news of farmers returning to their homes in Alexandria had reached her ears. People braced themselves for the winter with the warmth of peace at its core. But the nagging feeling that it was to be short-lived never left her in peace. It only felt like the deep silence before a storm. She sat there and saw Damian toil in the sparring session, a mild smile on her face.

"How can you still be sitting here?" An angry, yet soft voice startled her momentarily. She turned around to see the only relative from her father's side, a spitting image of her grandmother, also sharing her love for jewels. "Blessed morning, Aunt Isidora!"

"Don't you blessed morning me! Come with me, it's time to get you out of those filthy rags." Lysandra smiled at her concern. She was a wonderful lady, the guardian of Hydaspus after her husband passed away. Her son, Lysandra's cousin Leo was a part of the elite order of 'Southern Knights'.

"But it's only the fourth hour of the Sun," Lysandra was aghast.

"Yes, I am well aware of the time. Now off to the baths!"

"But my practice?" she quipped.

"You can do it after the ceremony. You are to be the youngest High Senator of Leu and think of the number of potential suitors. I was married and Leon was already in my womb when I was of your age," she said with pride, almost dragging Lysandra along.

"But Aunt Isidora, there are still a few days left," she protested.

"This is why I always told your father to remarry. A mother would have done you fine. You are a woman after all, and every eminent man of Leu will be there."

"They are coming for the ceremony, not me," stated Lysandra but was conveniently ignored.

"Not just spectators, family too! Lord Denis and the members of the Forest Hall, the Southern Knights," she continued animatedly, "Even the family of Lord Clitus and their young son Jason, eastern Lords, Lady Thales, Lady Nereus and her son Cleon....." She stopped and turned around, for Lysandra had stopped dead in her tracks.

"How is he?" she asked. Aunt Isidora saw her sad eyes and cursed her forgetfulness for having brought up his name.

"Cleon was fine when I saw him last. Now come," she coaxed but Lysandra did not move.

"Father never mentioned him in the guest list?"

"He is a Southern Knight now and as per tradition, must be called upon. There is nothing to mention here," chided Aunt Isidora.

"Yes, I understand." After some thought, she continued, "I have never met his wife; she must be beautiful." Her voice cracked for a moment and her aunt held her hand softly.

"My dear Lys, it was never about beauty. You are the fairest I have ever seen." She slowly caressed her cheeks. "Men often are afraid of women who tend to outdo them. In simple words, you were better than him and he knew that as well," said Aunt Isidora with sad eyes.

"He had promised to defend Leu with me, he had promised." Lysandra's eyes glistened with sorrow as Aunt Isidora embraced her.

"Men are good at breaking promises," her aunt said softly. "Some of them are reasons themselves while some have reasons. It is worth shedding tears for the later, love."

Lysandra closed her eyes, grief trickling down her cheeks.

▼

"Why wasn't I informed earlier?" Lysandra was furious.

She was seated with Torman and Damian. The High Sentry stammered, "I thought of informing you."

"Thought?...and then?" she raised an eyebrow. The man became more nervous.

"Yes, I did but the General said that you were busy preparing for the ceremony."

She cast a glance at Torman who looked away. She turned her attention to the High Sentry. "Next time onwards, you report to me. Soldiers of Leu getting attacked in broad daylight, that too in the capital, is something to be concerned about."

"But no one was killed," cut in Torman.

"And should we wait for that?" Lysandra snapped at Torman, who sunk his head in silence.

"And why have you not caught them yet?" she asked turning to the High Sentry.

"We are trying our best," replied the Sentry feverishly. "But they are crafty...The eyewitnesses say that one of them is very strong and he carries a black blade."

Lysandra was surprised.

"Yes, and horses have wings," chided Torman.

"Still, whatever it is, it's just one man," said Lysandra, surprised.

"We are short of men in the lower city. They hit and run," replied the man.

"Then take a few of the palace guards," Lysandra said matter-of-factly.

"Lys, is that wise?" whispered Damian. She did not reply.

"From today onwards, two regiments shall patrol the lower city. I want them caught, at any cost."

"Yes, Princess," said the High Sentry with a formal salute and left.

"Hope you know what you are doing," said Torman and walked out.

▼

The night slowly devoured the voices and the noises as she stood at the edge of the fall. The great mountain loomed behind her and the lower city below, dotted with tiny lights. There was no moon and the red sky hinted at a heavy rain. A cool breeze greeted her presence and she cuddled herself. Her eyes saw the southern horizon, pale and misty. If one could strain their eyes, the faint outline of Mount Lethe could be seen at dawn, but at night it remained invisible.

The open world made her feel free – free from thoughts souring her heart, free from bondages. She was ageing every day, more than others, and it had started from that very day when her heart had stopped beating.

"Isn't it a bit late to take a stroll in the garden, dear sister?" Damian spoke softly.

"Yes, I think so. But that didn't stop you, dear brother," she smiled.

"Yes," sighed Damian. "I get my bad habits from you."

"Really?" she laughed. "Then you are lucky and should be more thankful."

Damian's smile was warm and Lysandra couldn't help but confess, "I missed you. You gave me such a fright."

"That was one of those rare occasions when I scared myself," he smiled. "But seriously, the strangest part is I can't remember anything after the library."

She held his hand. "Then don't push yourself." Damian gave a nod.

"There is this deep-seated feeling... like something stirring in me," he took a deep breath, "...Thank the Maker that I am still here."

Lysandra was pleasantly surprised.

"Someone has changed." He smiled.

"There are better ways for a man to become a believer and I don't want Him teaching me any more lessons," he said sheepishly.

Lysandra's laughter was drowned by a loud scream reverberating through the palace. Lysandra was astounded. She looked at him. There was a hint of fear in Damian's eyes which she had never seen before.

▼

Damian and Lysandra ran towards the main gate. The shouts of battle were drawing louder and nearer. Then she saw Sophia, the maid running towards the guard's quarters.

"Intruders, Intruders....Palace Gate," Sophia screamed upon seeing them.

Damian caught hold of her. "Calm down Sophia. It's alright."

She gave a quick nod, her face white with fear.

"Sophia, Look at me!" Lysandra ordered. "How many are there?"

"Four or five maybe," she spoke with difficulty.

"Alright, now you run and wake the other guards," she commanded. The maid gave a nod and started running.

Lysandra lifted her night dress above her knees and tied it into a knot at her waist.

"Come brother," she said and rushed towards the gate.

"But how did they get inside?" Damian spoke out loud what had been bothering Lysandra too.

She kept mum for she knew that it had been a result of re-assigning most of the palace guards to the High Sentry. It had been a trap – all those attacks on the soldiers in the lower city – to reduce the security of the palace. But who would dare? There could be only one answer – the enemy was here.

They reached the grounds and saw the guards engaged in a heated skirmish with four hooded men, while one stood at a distance.

She picked up a sword from the ground and rushed towards what seemed like the leader. But to her surprise, one of the four broke away from the battle and stood in front of her.

She charged with all ferocity and swung her blade wildly, but it was stopped. Her eyes became wide for the blade that had stopped hers was jade black. She gathered herself and pushed on but the hooded man matched each step.

"You are quite adept with your sword," spoke a voice.

"You think a woman can't fight?" she barked and continued her assault.

"You are mistaken. You are efficient, and you are a woman; that makes you an exceptional foe," he replied, which surprised her a bit and slowed her down for a split second.

The man took that opportunity and pushed her blade with his. The gown came loose and made her trip. She felt the searing heat of the blade on her throat.

"Princess," called out one of the guards and rushed towards her, followed by Damian.

"Princess?" repeated the man and she felt the sword retreating.

"Stop!" he shouted and the others retreated as well.

"Our intention is not to harm anyone. We only want to speak to your King," said the man, his deep blue eyes pouring into hers.

She quickly got up and placed her blade on his throat.

"How dare you?" she shouted. "You harmed the soldiers of Leu and broke into the royal palace. Give me one good reason that I shouldn't kill you right here."

The man took down his hood, and she saw that he was almost of the same age as hers.

"I will give you two. First, I couldn't come through the front door; your father will understand. And second, your father has been expecting me for a very long time for...," he paused and let the revelation sink in, "...my name is Agni. I am the son of King Arkansas."

Agni's Quest
(The Land of the Rising Sun)

(The story resumes from a year back from the recent events just after Agni's escape from Nisarga.)

The whirling smoke from the cheroot was dissipated by the howling wind. His deep blue eyes drank the beauty bestowed to the mountains by the rising sun. The ice caps covering the peaks glistened, separated from the tracts of greenery by the floating clouds. Yet, all the beauty of nature couldn't fill his emptiness. Mount Gumbaj gave him little solace.

"It's beautiful here, isn't it?" asked Vrish.

"Yes, as much as it could be," replied Agni as he flicked the ash. His unkempt hair and unshaved face made him look blanch. He pursed his cracked lips from time to time.

They had been travelling for the past few days with a pack of hermits to avoid unnecessary attention. A chant rose in the air and the duo glanced back. Sidak and Param were with them as well.

"There they go again," said Vrish and looked away.

'At least they have a way to come to terms with their past,' thought Agni as they saw the hermits offering food to their ancestors.

"Param said that we will cross over the mountain in a few days and reach the outskirts of Aadhar, but..."

Agni already knew what he was going to say. They couldn't go back to Himadri for it'd be the first place they would be looked for. What they had stolen would have been discovered by then. So the plan was to lay low in Kyat until Sidak deciphered the scroll. But all that seemed meaningless to him.

"What are you thinking?" asked Vrish.

"Nothing," replied Agni. "Sometimes it is hard to live with oneself."

"You did not choose this. *We* did not choose this," said Vrish.

"What difference does it make? One way or the other, the reason remains the same," replied Agni nonchalantly. Then he looked at Vrish and said, "If I were in your shoes, I would have left by now."

"I do not see it like that," Vrish said quietly. "The way I see it – fate is cruel."

"Her death was not her fate," spat back Agni. "This was not supposed to be our fate."

"She was my sister, Agni, and I lost my father too," replied Vrish. Agni did not look at him in the eye.

"And I am to be blamed for that," he confessed, more to himself.

He felt Vrish's hand on his shoulder. "You have given it more than you had. It was a never a choice. Now you and I have nothing left, except each other. There is nothing to forgive my dear friend. It would be better if we start forgetting what happened, because it will take a long time."

Agni looked at him, his heart was crying, but his tears had dried up.

Vrish continued in a soft voice, "You loved her more than any man ever could. She rests in peace, Agni." May be it is time to lose that," said Vrish pointing at his pocket. Agni felt Malini's pendant on his fingertips as his hand slipped inside his pocket. The sheer thought of even misplacing this prized possession gave him a shudder.

The chant rose to its highest pitch and drew their attention. "I asked Param last night about what they sing," said Vrish.

"What did he tell you?" asked Agni, hiding away from the painful thoughts.

"They sing that, 'home is never lost unless you lose the way on your own; it is not always made of bricks but where someone is waiting for you. They have lost theirs to the darkness and where stood their little hovels now stand a maze of lies. But they will continue their search. The hills shall call them back again. For home is not made of bricks; it is where love is'."

▼

Lord Kubha was pacing to and fro, his anxious eyes glued to the kitchen door. It was cold inside with the servants away, yet he sweated profusely. The sentries stood in silence.

The door opened and the armed preachers walked in, led by a man-servant. Lord Kubha smiled at them, but they stood there motionless and their faces were devoid of any expression. Their clean shaved heads with ponytails, draped in white and brazened faces made him sweat some more.

A few moments later, a tall and well built man with a cruel face walked in; he was dressed in saffron.

"Guru Bodhan, it is an honour to be in your presence again. I hope the journey was well and I would have met you at the gates if I had known that you were coming."

A hallowed pair of eyes fell on Kubha and he went silent.

"Lead us to that place," spoke the man without banter.

"As you say," said Kubha and opened the door of the storeroom.

"Tell your men to stay back," said Bodhan as he entered the dark and damp room.

Kubha gave a nod with some hesitation. The sentries closed the door.

There was complete darkness. The nebulous outlines of the two preachers seemed to take something out from the folds of their clothes. They threw something in the air and to Kubha's surprise it illuminated the room. The dust was in the air was emitting a white radiance.

Guru Bodhan stood in front of a wall and did something. A door appeared out of nowhere which opened into a tunnel.

"Follow my lead," said the Guru and walked into the tunnel, closely followed by the preachers. Kubha had little choice.

What followed was a long and exhaustive walk through the tunnels in complete silence. Bodhan led them through one obstacle to another with ease. It seemed like a bad dream to Kubha and then after a long and weary journey through the devouring darkness, they found themselves in a circular hall with a sarcophagus in the middle. Its lid was removed and under it was a dead body while another lay a few feet away. The sceptre was fixated on one side of the sarcophagus.

"Is this place...?" paused Kubha, perspiring profusely.

"For a fool, ignorance can be bliss; but you fail at proving yourself that too," replied Bodhan.

"I did not know," Kubha was horrified. "Had I known, I would have never given away the sceptre. I sent word to you as soon as I came to know myself; then those things, they came out of nowhere," his voice was trembling.

"A bleating sheep mistook itself for a fierce tiger and now its fate hangs in balance."

Kubha was petrified. He felt his knees go weak.

"Please, please forgive me. I was asked to pass on the sceptre as the heirloom of my house and that is what I tried to do. Tell me what to do to mend all this, and you will not have an opportunity to doubt me," he sobbed.

Bodhan was unabashed. "Pray, pray to the Trinetra that we find the boy."

▼

"I do not think I can do this. What if the word escapes? Then all shall lay in ruin. My family, my kingdom and even the reputation of my house," said one man.

"Does your wife know?" asked another.

"No."

"Now is not the time to think back, Raja! We had decided on it. I have placed everything on the line based on your word," said the third man.

The man they were addressing gave a slight nod.

"You have nothing to lose and what will happen when you will grow old? Your name shall be diminished to nothing and your line shall come to an end."

The man came up and put his hand on the Raja's shoulder.

"It is for the best. We all love our sons and you shall have just the one you wished for. Your lineage shall continue."

The Raja gave a final nod, and the man nodded in agreement.

"Come sage; let us not keep our sailor friend waiting."

Then the image disappeared in a flash and a thousand flashes blinded Agni's gaze. He woke up with a jerk, his fingers burning over the blade. The blade was oozing steam. He was about to say something when a Sidak's fingers sealed his lips, "We have visitors."

▼

Agni sat up and found himself in the cover of the shrubs at the edge of the river of Sheetaldhara.

"We tried to wake you, but you just didn't hear us. So we had to move you here. You were clutching onto that thing and wouldn't let go," whispered Vrish.

Agni looked at his hand, his fingers were blackened. Then he looked straight and saw four horsemen standing a few paces away, questioning the hermits.

"Are they from Nisarga?" asked Agni.

Sidak hesitated for a moment and responded in a hush, "No."

"Then why are we hiding?"

"They are the Nimit," replied Sidak without looking.

"The Nimit?" questioned Agni, and saw the riders disappear in the darkness of the night.

Sidak walked out of the bush but did not go out in the open. "We better wait here for some time, in case they decide to come back," he said, caution clear in his words.

Agni looked at Vrish, "What is the Nimit? he asked looking at Sidak.

Sidak was staring at him, and then he dropped his gaze. Agni could see he was in two minds. "There is no use in keeping it from you now," Sidak said after a brief pause. "It is better that I tell you now than later, in case we run into them again."

Agni had a feeling of apathy growing in him as Sidak spoke, "The Nimit is an old order; they are the guardians of the Secret of Nisarga."

"Guardians? I thought the scroll was a secret itself?" asked Vrish.

"It is, and only a very few know of it. They are those who protect it. It is the pact with the Abode forged long back during the days of Darshana himself. The Nimit protect the scroll and in lieu, the Abode does not interfere in the matters of the Land of the Rising Sun. That's why they are searching for the scroll, and will continue doing so until it is found. They are the ones to hide from; mere soldiers won't matter... That is why the key was broken into two parts and secret hidden by the three disciples – my ancestor, General Cabasa and the jewel of the east, Opalina."

Agni felt his anger rising. "And you did not bother to tell us all this before?"

"I wanted to reach Kyat first. I never thought they would try to find us here," replied Sidak.

"Great! Now we have an ancient order chasing us as well," grumbled Vrish. Then he looked at Sidak and said, "Next time onwards, do make a list of priorities."

"My priority is to protect you two, that's all," replied Sidak with indifference.

"Why?" shouted Agni. "You have your scroll. Why do you need us?"

"Because that was what I promised your father." Sidak placed a hand on his shoulder. "Don't you see, Agni? Your father was a drop in the ocean that created a ripple. We are bound, our freedom has been taken away; and he wanted to change that. Fate chose you to finish what he started."

Agni removed his hand and looked straight at him. "Get one thing straight, Guruji! I am not in this to find any secrets. I don't give a rat's ass as to what fate wants me to do. All I want to know is what happened to my family. Who betrayed my father and where my... where my mother is. Or if she is alive or not."

Sidak smiled. "Either way, our roads are the same."

"For now," replied Agni.

Sidak gave a nod. "For now." He agreed.

The Shrouded Past
(The Land of the Rising Sun)

The Tale of Charvi

The city of Anu, one of the oldest cities in the Land of the Rising Sun, was famous for its scholars and their myriad ways to feats worthy of Gaya's notice. Yet there existed a small problem which hindered some – the religious rigidity of the higher class. It is here, where the great scholar Aca was born who developed the concept of 'void', the theory of complete emptiness where things existed in different forms.

The city roads were empty and the full moon lent white light to the city along with the lanterns. The Aranyapath ran from Uttarbhumi (North City) to Dakshinbhumi (South City) with the forest 'Dash hastha' in between. The patrols were in plenty despite the fact that the city had the lowest crime rate than any other city of Gaya.

A small figure with a satchel strapped around her back walked down Aranyapath. The guards caste a few suspicious looks but did not hinder her when their eyes fell on the books clutched in her hand. Gurus were held in high esteem in Anu.

The girl appeared within a bell hour in front of the wooden door of a small house in Uttarbhumi. She knocked on the door softly. A few moments passed before the sour rattled voice, laced with heavy undertone of age, called out, "Who is it?"

"It's me Guruji, Charvi," replied the girl softly.

The door opened and an old man stepped out with a lamp in his hand. "Charvi!" he exclaimed. "What are you doing here at this hour? Is everything alright?"

"Yes Guruji, everything is fine."

Then he peeked over her shoulder. "I do not see any carriage, how did you get here?" he asked.

"I walked," she replied happily.

"You what?" he asked repulsed.

""Can I come inside first?"

The old Guru, Marut, stood there speechless. "Yes," he replied gathering himself.

She walked in following the old man.

"That was reckless Charvi. Whatever it was, you should have come in the morning. The roads are not as safe as they used to be."

The girl stood there smiling. Marut was confused.

"What is so amusing?"

"I think I have found something."

""What?" asked the old man, more confused than before.

"I will show you," she said unclasping her satchel. She scurried through the books inside. "For the last few days I have been plagued by officials wanting to go through my father's scrolls, again."

"And why is that?" asked Marut, stressed. "We solved that problem long ago."

"They said that it was directly ordered by the 'Mantri parishad'."

"Why did you not inform me earlier?" enquired an agitated Marut.

She grinned in return. "Nonetheless, I started going through them myself, as to see if I had missed something. If they are still at it then they must think that my father had left behind something." Marut did not seem pleased.

"Remember, that puzzle of numbers and symbols I showed you earlier in my father's journal?" she said looking up.

"Not that again. I have told you many times Charvi that the Cipher is incomplete. It needs a key," replied an irritated Marut.

"Exactly and that is what I have to say." She quickly took out a bundle of pages. "I went through each and every book of my father's library and I found one separate page stitched randomly to each book. I tore them out and arranged them in numerical order. There are seven hundred and sixty nine pages."

She handed them over to Marut.

"It is written in Chhanda," said Marut, astonished.

"Yes and the red marks on some of them are in direct relation to the numbers."

Marut went through the pages one by one. "But there is one missing." Marut turned over another page and then his eyes became vivid. "Did you find all this in your father's library?"

"Yes and not only that, I found something else as well."

"Charvi," cut in Marut. "Do you have the slightest idea as to what this is?"

Charvi shook her head.

Marut closed his eyes. "I thought so. Wait here," he said and walked inside. He came out within a moment with another book in his hand. He laid it open in front of her. "This is the re-written work of Darshana, one of the rarest of the rare books."

Then he took the torn pages and opened the book. He placed each page on another identical one, except a few which contained hand-drawn pictures, the ones marked.

"Now do you understand?" he asked gruffly.

"It's the original work of Darshana himself," she looked up, her eyes shining.

"One of the three. The only difference between the re-written ones and the three originals are the pictures."

"Now I understand. May be that is why he had marked them with red. May be they form a part of the Cipher like I thought!" she exclaimed excitedly.

"Charvi," barked Marut. "Don't you understand the seriousness of this matter? Can you imagine the consequences if this is discovered?"

"No one has to know, Guruji."

Marut gave a sigh.

"You father meddled in things which he shouldn't have, and now this. You walk on the same path not knowing where it might lead you."

"Guruji, I understand what you mean to say. But I have firm faith he left this to us for some reason."

"And he did not return for the very same," Marut spat back.

Charvi went silent. Marut felt bad for her, even pity. He took her hand in his. "Don't you understand your father's folly dear Charvi? He was my student and I, his teacher. He was bright like you but still there are a few things which should not be trifled with, because the results can be terrible."

Charvi retracted her hand. "Is this one of them?" She asked as she took an odd object, grotesque in looks. It seemed like a thin bird, a pole jutting out from the centre with three flat blades attached to the top.

"And what might this be?" asked Marut exasperated.

"I will show you," she said and started rotating a knob attached to its side.

When she let go, the thing lifted to the air all by itself. Marut was stunned. It whirled around and landed on the ground.

"I, I don't understand. How?" He picked it up in his hand. "It is made of wood," he said looking at her. "But how can wood fly like this?"

"I found it in one of the hidden cases under the shelves. I believe it was made by him."

Marut kept on staring at her foolishly.

"Now do you understand, Guruji, why my father left me and my mother twenty years back, when I was still inside her womb! If pursuit of knowledge was more important to him than his daughter, then I want to know what this knowledge is."

Her eyes were fixed on his, Marut saw the same dreaded determination in her eyes aswell.

▼

Charvi was waiting outside Gyanlok, the centre of learning and the famed seat of knowledge of Anu, presided over by Rishi Bhavesh.

She looked around and saw young men and women engaged in fearsome duels in the sparing grounds. Her attention was diverted by throng of bows; Anu had always excelled in bowman-ship (*dhanushvidya*).

"Charvi," called out Marut and gestured her to follow.

She walked in small steps behind him.

"Remember Charvi, Rishi Bhavesh is not only a guru but a *rishi* (saint) as well. He is the spiritual advisor in the royal court, second to none but the Maharaj himself. If anyone can help you, it is he. So touch his feet on your first formal greeting." Charvi nodded.

They walked inside the modest edifice, a simple structure of wood and brick. The *shlokas* and the chants of old were engraved on the brick wall with gold dust, and tapestries sewn from silver thread adorned the place. She paused to marvel at the subtle beauty of the sanctum.

"Charvi," called Marut and she followed hurriedly.

Marut took off his slippers and entered the room. She followed suit to enter.

It was an open court of sorts that was supported by six pillars. In the centre sat Guru Bhavesh, dressed in simple saffron silks, his hair braided and strings of holy beads coiled around his arms. In comparison to him, she was dressed better, in a cream sari, her curly black locks kneaded in a decent knot which complimented her sharp nose, small lips and dreamy eyes.

"Rishiji, this is Charvi." She stepped forward and touched his feet.

"It seems that humility and beauty goes hand in hand," paused Rishi Bhavesh. "And you have also taught her well."

Marut folded his hands and gave a small bow in return of the good gesture.

"So you are Charvi, daughter of Aranya?" he asked.

She merely nodded.

"Find voice young one. You have nothing to fear here."

"Yes Rishiji," said Charvi meekly.

"Good."

"Your Guruji says that you have something to share which is worth Anu's attention?" His piercing eyes were fixed on her.

Charvi nodded again.

"Good, very good. Anu has always celebrated new talents and she shall continue doing so. Show me then."

"Do what you did earlier Charvi," urged Marut.

Charvi took out the flying device and rotated its knob like before. The results were the same; it took to the air and landed softly after a while. She had a smile on her face, but it changed as she saw the dour look on the old Rishi's face.

"Marut, you know very well that sorcery is not tolerated in Anu," said Rishi Bhavesh coldly.

"But this is not sorcery, Rishiji," replied Charvi promptly.

"Silence, young one! It is not you whom I speak to."

Marut was disquieted for the moment at the sudden turn of events. But he found his voice.

"She is speaking the truth, Rishiji. I believe this to be an advanced device of sorts, which with the right application can solve the riddle of flight."

"If so, then why hasn't any greater mind of Anu claimed this yet? The ones with touch of divinity and the greatness of experience," asked Rishi Bhavesh glowering.

"One greater mind has," she replied and started to chant.

"I have seen the stars, the greater darkness of beyond,

Where sight slowly fades yet the heart grows fond.

Glimpses of wingless ones, made neither of flesh or magic, took to the air,

They raced the wind as they rained down fire.

Verse 372 of the book of Darshana," she finished.

"And how do you know this?" breathed the old Rishi. Charvi remained silent.

"I knew it; you walk the same twisted path as your father. Eccentrics and fanatics dream of many twisted dreams but that does turn them into reality. Your father being the brightest of Anu failed to understand this. Man is made by Trinetra himself. If they were to fly then the great one would have blessed them with wings."

"So you can explain why he didn't give us gills and yet we sail the seas," Charvi was quick.

Rishi Bhavesh's face became twisted and his eyes vented deep-seeded fury.

"Charvi," cautioned Marut quickly.

"How dare you? How dare you challenge the wisdom of ages?" roared the old sage. "Your father was an insolent fool like you and he breathed his last before his due."

Charvi's eyes were red. Yet she drew a deep breath and turned around. "It seems I have come to the wrong place to seek answers."

She started walking.

"Your father chased after these mad ideas and lost his way. You shall suffer the same fate," cursed the old Rishi.

"So be it," she replied calmly.

Marut quickly followed her outside. "What have you done, child?" said the old Marut with a hint of fear in his voice.

She paused. "Now I understand why my father wrote in his journal that the answers lie in the Land of the Setting Sun."

"And what do you mean by that?" asked Marut, petrified.

Charvi closed her eyes, trying not to match her Guru's gaze. "I have decided Guruji; I am going to the Land of the Setting Sun. I am going to Leu. I will follow his path."

▼

Charvi's eyes were glued to the porch leading to the door. She awaited Marut's arrival and it was becoming unbearable. Her master had gone seeking a permit from the Lok Parishad which would allow Charvi to travel to the Land of the Setting Sun. Without it, she couldn't go onboard any listed vessel in any port city except pirate ports. Marut was trying to use his connections to get her one. Her heart jumped as she saw Marut return. She ran out on the porch.

"Did it work?" she asked enthusiastically, but Marut gently shook his head. Her heart sank.

"They don't want you to leave, or so it seems. I think after that incident, you will be investigated," replied Marut.

"Then what do we do now?" asked Charvi with a pensive look on her face.

Marut remained silent. He himself did not have any answer.

The Journey Back Home
(The Land of the Rising Sun)

"Are you certain about this, Agni?" asked Sidak.
"Yes, I am. If I am to know the truth, then I shall have to go back where it all started," he replied. Sidak was staring at him. Somehow he found this Agni more confident and poised. This time he was not driven by hate.

He stood up and smiled. "There is an old saying; the more you try to avoid your destiny the closer you get to it. Your father wanted you away from that place, and you wish to go there by will."

"I cannot run forever, Guruji," said Agni and then he looked at Vrish. "We cannot run forever."

Vrish seemed thoughtful, "But how are we going to do this? We can't just march into Athena, that is where we will need help."

"Vrish is right. Even I do not know anyone there," stated Sidak.

"Well I have thought of an idea. Solon mentioned someone named King Crixus and he was a good friend of my father's. We can go to him."

"Yes, I have heard of King Crixus of Leu from your father as well. But there is a slight problem there," said Sidak drawing their attention. "How are you going to convince the man that you are his friend's son? You do not bear his name, neither the title nor sigil, and the West is very different Agni. You are not supposed to be alive. We don't even know how the man will react."

"Guruji has a point," said Vrish.

Agni was engrossed in thinking a way out when his face suddenly lit up, "The letter! The letter that my father left in Adhirath's hand for Solon. It is a proof of my identity and it bears his seal."

"But was not Solon the one who last possessed it?" asked Sidak.

"True but there can be another answer as well. After handing over the letter, Solon had used the information about Yani to coax Adhirathji into helping him. So, the latter would have become aware as to what information the letter contained."

"And the way that man is, he mustn't have allowed the letter to slip out of Himadri," added Vrish.

"Exactly," cut in Agni. "And I bet he still has that letter."

Sidak was sitting there, his fingers tightly clasped together. "Hmmm, you have a point, but it is only a hunch. What if you are wrong? The city will be heavily guarded and the King, more so. The Nimit must have spun some tales about you already and also," Sidak paused, "you are going to ask the man to give up his greatest secret."

"I don't see any other choice," replied Agni firmly.

"There is also another problem. How are we going to get inside Himadri?" asked Sidak.

Agni was a bit surprised. "I thought you could get us inside the city easily."

Sidak shook his head. "Adhirath must have noticed my absence by now. Even if he hasn't, I can't take that risk because we could walk right into a trap that way."

When Vrish also shrugged indicating his helplessness, Agni slumped on the grass. "Then we have a problem," he admitted.

"Just when we thought we had something. If the dockhands wouldn't have been such religious folks then we could have had a chance in entering from sea," grumbled Vrish.

"What do you mean? asked Agni.

"Tirthayatras (religious travel), they must have already gone for the yatra," replied Vrish.

"Of course," said Agni and stood up. "There is the season of Tirthayatras; there will be a thousand travellers at least and they all shall go to Himgiri through Himadri." Seeing the blank faces of the other two, he quickly added, "We can easily use that to our advantage."

Realisation struck Vrish and he cut in, "Yes! Not all the yatris have permits, and the guards let them pass after they fish out some ginis from their pockets."

Sidak was smiling. Agni never failed to amaze him. "Then we shall need some saffron clothes and offering pots," he said at last. Seeing Agni's broad smile, he added, "I shall talk to the hermits to see whether they have some extra clothes." He turned to Vrish. "You go and find Param, he shall know where to find offering pots."

"Alright," said Vrish and started walking. Sidak stood up as well. Agni saw Vrish disappear in the lush outgrowth of trees.

"Guruji! Can I have a word with you?" said Agni.

"Of course."

Agni hesitated for a moment. "Tell Agni," he insisted.

"Did you know of Solon's plan to kill Briksha?"

Sidak was silent. "Yes," he replied after a brief pause. Agni's face turned sour.

"You are a guru, didn't it bother you?" The bitterness in his voice was clear.

"Frankly, I did not know that Solon would harm the girl as well," replied Sidak.

"Her name is Malini," barked Agni.

There were a few moments of silence as the world spun in its own speed.

"If you think that I am to blame for her death, even partly, then you are sorely mistaken Agni. Your father made Solon your guardian, not me, and he did what he thought was best."

"Killing an innocent to save another," Agni spat back.

"Then I will say something on Solon's stead. When the line between morals and duty gets blurred, then it is better to rub it off yourself than waiting for someone else to do it for you. In the real world, secrets cost more than just turmoil and vexation. Either way, the choice is dead," replied Sidak calmly.

"There is always a choice," Agni uttered each word with great belief.

"Better men in the eyes of Trinetra have better choices, but not all are so lucky."

▼

The horizon lighted up in an orange tinge as the red ball of fire slowly crept out from the mist. Agni and the others had camped on the grounds outside the gate with the other yatris. They had become one with the crowd. The unkempt hair, unshaved faces and the dirty saffron clothes hid any connections with royalty and made them appear as mere commoners.

"The gates are opening," Param called back from the front. They had split into two groups to avoid notice. Agni's eyes were on the duo in the front while Vrish walked beside him.

"Is there something wrong, Agni," he asked confused, "between you and Sidak?"

"My trust on that man is waning. He knew of Solon's intentions of burning Dut, yet he did nothing," replied Agni.

Vrish's face was devoid of any expression but there was a hint of surprise. "I did guess that or rather you can say that I knew somehow."

Agni was astounded. "Yet you said nothing of it to me."

"Sometimes I just do not know what to feel nowadays. I only wish I could stop thinking," Vrish seemed defeated on that front.

"He knew that your father and your sister were going to die and yet you forgive him that easily," said Agni with spite.

Vrish stopped. "Who said anything about forgiveness?" There was a hint of anger in his voice. "We are with this man because we don't have a choice. That is all I know. I want to believe that everything passes away, so did my father and my sister. But it's hard, very hard. They are gone, Agni, and Solon is dead. I just want all this to end. What more can I say?"

"Then why are you with me, Vrish? You still have a way out," said Agni calmly. Vrish had a defiant smile on his face.

"You know answer to that or at least you once did."

▼

The crowd was rushing forward as if the Himgiri would float away if they delayed even one bit. He lost Vrish in the crowd, but it was Himadri, and he need not worry. Vrish knew his way better than anyone else in there. He was inside after a few routine stares from the gatekeeper. Then he was asked to make an offering and he fished out a mudra. The gatekeeper allowed him inside with a hint of a smile on his face. Agni saw the high tower looming on the other side and gave a sigh of relief. He saw Param and Sidak at a distance with the former waving at him. He looked around but couldn't see Vrish.

There was hue and cry at the gate and Agni turned to see that the travellers had halted. His heart skipped a bit as he turned around and ran. There was something happening under the portcullis. Agni peered over the crowd and saw Vrish arguing with the gatekeeper.

"How dare you deny the gift of passage? You either give that or get lost," the angry words of the gatekeeper floated to his ears.

"You take all the ginis if you want, but not this," said Vrish firmly. The man held on his wrist with a firm grip.

"Let go," threatened Vrish.

"Or what?" shouted the man, drizzling spit on his face. The fingers on his other hand curled into a fist, but Agni caught it before he could lift it.

Vrish glowered at him.

"Give the good man what he wants, dear friend. We are going to God's own realm in Gaya. Why fight?" said Agni, his eyes fixed on Vrish.

"And who the hell are you?' barked the gatekeeper. "How dare you interfere in this?"

Agni softened his gaze. "Just a fellow yatri, Rakshakji. Met him on the road. He is from the mountains and doesn't know the ways of the city," bleated Agni.

"The fool from the mountain," sneered the man and the other guards smiled.

Vrish cast his friend a sour look.

"Open your hand my friend," Agni almost pleaded.

Vrish was staring at him with sad eyes and then he slowly opened his hand. To Agni's surprise, there was a thin shinning gold chain in it.

The man snatched it from his hand.

"That's a good boy."

"Can we go now, Rakshakji?" asked Agni.

"Yeah, why not," said the gatekeeper. Then he looked at Vrish and smiled, "Fuckers like you should stay where they belong. And why carry such a trinket?"

Vrish stopped. His eyes fixed on the man. Agni tried to drag him.

"Maybe I know," smiled the gatekeeper. "Want to shove this in some whore's..."

The gatekeeper fell on the ground, his nose bleeding. Vrish had punched him before he could finish.

"Kill that bastard," the gatekeeper screamed. While the other travellers started running.

Agni noticed the gatekeeper's purse on the table and went for it. He threw the coins in the air before the others could come. Some of the yatris jumped at it and it all turned to chaos.

He dragged Vrish along from under the portcullis.

"Here," came Sidak's voice and they started to run towards the alley. Agni did not look back. The moments passed by with the breeze. They were in some garden in the eastern section of the city.

"What is wrong with you?" shouted Agni. "You couldn't even take an insult, huh?" he shouted.

"Don't speak of what you don't know," replied Vrish calmly and started walking.

"Don't you dare walk away. You put us all in danger back there," shouted Agni as he tried to grab Vrish.

Vrish shoved his hand away and turned around. "Keep your hands to yourself!" warned Vrish.

"What are you going to do? Punch me as well?" he shouted.

"I think you two should stop this," cut in Sidak.

"You stay out of this," pointed Agni at Sidak. He became silent but his gaze remained unmoved.

"You are pathetic," chided Vrish.

"Am I?" Agni pushed him. "Or are you the one? Oh right, I forgot. You don't know what to think these days? Right?"

Vrish clenched his fists. "Who the fuck do you think you are? You want us to kill every man who knew about the fire. You think you have lost it all."

He put his finger on Agni's chest and continued enraged, "I have lost my family. You wanted to marry her and that's all. You can marry someone else for all I know, but can I get a new sister or a father. Can I?"

Agni was fuming but Vrish did not let him speak, "You want to know why I fought for that chain. It was my mother's and it was supposed to be my gift of gold to Bani if she would have accepted it after knowing the entire truth. Then I would have left with you."

Agni was staring at him. "Vrish," he spoke with nonchalance, "I don't give a damn."

Vrish took a step back. "I know, and that is why you will be alone, just as you always were."

"Get lost," were Agni's words.

Vrish turned around, cast one final glance at Agni and started walking.

"I know that you asked me not to interfere but that was not the right thing to do," said Sidak.

Agni cast him a glance and saw him walking away as well, followed by Param. He stood there in the middle, alone. His heart was beating frantically. He was engulfed by a strange fear he could not understand.

He slowly closed his eyes.

"Malini," he whispered to himself, the blinding flashes cindering his heart.

Shadows of the past
(The Land of the Rising Sun)

The tale of Charvi

Charvi sat pouring over her father's journal. There was a strange symbol on the cover which she had shown to Marut — the four hands pointing neither north, nor south, not east or west with a bisected square in the middle.

Marut had asked her to hide everything, specially the pages which she had discovered. So she kept herself busy sorting them out for specific hiding spots.

Her eyes fell on the scroll in which her father had written down the cipher.

The same symbol was on the top of the scroll as well and below was etched the set of numbers along with fourteen rectangles at the bottom.

From what she had made out from the recent discovery of Darshan's authentic work, it seemed that the second set of numbers denoted the hand drawn images of Darshana's journey to the Land beyond the Wall or The Land of Demons as most commonly called. But what the other set of numbers signified remained a mystery to her, yet. The biggest question in her mind was that even if this was a cipher, what was it meant to unlock?

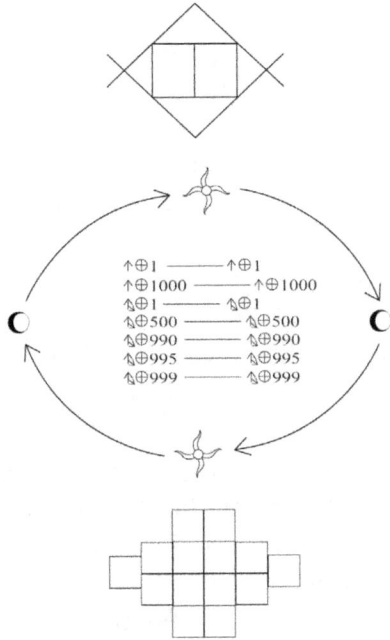

The questions started to swarm in her head, and frustrated, she closed the scroll.

Then suddenly there was a faint noise coming from the stairs. She listened carefully. There was nothing. It was an old house which cracked and groaned with the wind. Her father had left behind many things and this old villa was one of them.

After her mother had passed away a few years back, the sheer emptiness of the house used to frighten her, but she had grown accustomed to it with time.

There it was again, much more definitive and clearer than before.

'Burglars' was her first thought, though it was uncommon in Anu, yet a large villa under the care of an old servant and young girl had drawn the wrong attention before. Old Shankar being away, it would have been the perfect opportunity for brigands. She quickly put the scroll and the pages in the satchel and blew out the candle.

Footsteps were now as loud as drum beats. "Thieves won't come to a library," she consoled herself as she hid behind one of the shelves.

Two men walked in slowly, one lean and the other fat.

"You said you saw light up here?" asked one of them.

"I think I did," replied the other. Charvi quickly crawled under one of the shelves. Within moments she saw a pair of feet pass by.

"Damn those bearded shits, some low life could have handled this job but they had to ruin our night," complained the lean one.

"Keep your fucking voice low, what if she hears us?" whispered the other one angrily.

Charvi's heart started to beat frantically. The word 'she' rang in her ears. They were not random burglars.

"Mother, help me," she whispered to herself.

"I will go and check the other side. You finish up here," said one of them, the lean one.

"Why not!" said the other one glumly.

Then to her horror, she heard the creaking of wood. The man was knocking on the wood to find hollow spots and it was only a matter of time before she was discovered.

Her eyes frantically searched for a way out and then she saw the window, a few paces to her left. If she tried to make a dash for it, she would most certainly be noticed.

There was only one thing to do. There was only one of them and if she could buy some time, she could make it out before the other one came back. The library was on the first floor but she would have to take that chance. She crawled out slowly and lifted one of the heavier metal encasements.

A peep through the gaps showed that the man was nearby, inspecting the shelves a few paces away.

'My fate is mine and I can change it,' she recollected her father's words from the journal.

The footsteps were drawing nearer.

'Mother! Give me strength.' Her fingers tightened around the metal. Her whole body was shaking. The man was close, barely a few steps away. She could feel it. Beads of sweat trickled down her brow.

"Hey, over here," came the other voice and the footsteps stopped.

"What is it?" asked the other one.

"One of the rooms in the west wing is bolted from the inside. I think she is inside."

'Trinetra bless Shankar. He always used to bolt his door from the inside and use the servant's exit in the basement whenever he left for long. He was a man of privacy,' thought Charvi.

The footsteps were becoming distant and then she heard them disappear down the stairs. She peeped out and saw nothing. Charvi ran and squeezed herself out of the window, and stood on the ledge of the shed of the veranda. The ground seemed far away, but she had little choice. She closed her eyes and jumped. An agonising pain ran up her spine. She put her hand on her mouth and a muffled groan escaped.

Her ankle was sprained. But she forced herself up and started to limp her way out of the yards.

"She is escaping," came the frantic gibber of one of the assassins.

The satchel was dangling from her back, and she looked back once. She could make out two shadowy figures by the window, and then they disappeared.

She did not look back again and forced her legs to speed up. But they were failing her. Then the light of the lantern at the far end of the road became visible, the night patrol was near. She put in all her effort to reach them; she was almost there.

▼

"Is it paining still?" Marut's voice floated to her ears. Charvi was lost in her thoughts, the lamp flickered with the night wind and the pitch black darkness had consumed the world around them. The grey outlines hinting their whimsical ways.

She jumped back to reality.

"No, Guruji. It's fine now."

"The salve is working. I will wrap it with linen and wood. It will be easier for you to walk."

"I can do that, Guruji," replied a discomforted Charvi.

Marut smiled. "There is no shame for a disciple to be treated for her injuries. Touching your feet will not lessen your respect for me in your heart."

She gave a weak nod. Marut sat down with some difficulty and started applying the salve.

"Now tell me, did you get a good look at their faces?"

"It was dark Guruji," she replied meekly.

"Hmm," Marut nodded. "The strangest thing is that they escaped despite being surrounded by the patrol and they didn't take anything from the house."

Marut finished bandaging her feet. "Now, this must serve as a lesson to you. Trinetra forbid, you could have gone through worse. You should have done what I had told you earlier. Sell the house and I will help you find one near mine. This neighbourhood is one of the safest in the city and the people are good too. One simple shout for help will bring many over in no time."

The old guru kept talking and when he looked up, he saw an unmindful Charvi staring outside the window.

"Charvi!" called out Marut softly. "Is everything alright?"

She pursed her lips, the mark of hesitation on her face was as clear as dawn.

"What is it child? You can tell me."

She looked up, still hesitant. "There is something I did not tell the Rakshaks."

Marut remained silent, the anticipation clear on his face.

"They weren't burglars Guruji, they came for me. I heard them say it."

Marut was stunned, he sat there frozen.

"I am sorry Guruji," apologized Charvi. "I didn't want you to worry."

The compelling silence and the chant of the wind were broken by the loud barking of strays.

Charvi looked outside the window.

"Don't," Marut almost shouted. She was startled by his sudden outburst.

The old guru quickly stood up and closed the window. He advanced to bolt the door from inside.

"What are you doing Guruji?"

Marut did not reply. The door of the almirah was opened rather rashly.

"Guruji?" called out Charvi again. "What are you doing?"

The dogs screamed as if hit by something and the doldrums faded away.

He paused for a moment and then took out something hastily from the almirah. There was a black cylindrical object in his hand, barely a few inches long.

"Hold this Charvi, and keep it safe. They must be outside by now. We will wait for the moment and then make our gateway."

Charvi was scared. She caught hold of Marut's hand.

"What is going on Guruji? You are scaring me. Who is outside?"

Marut seemed to have aged twenty years within moments.

"We don't have time for this, please," he pleaded.

"No, what are you hiding? Tell me or else I shall go outside and see for myself."

Marut lowered his gaze.

"This has happened before."

"What?" she asked blankly.

"Your father had a way of life. He used to meddle in things he shouldn't have. Lastly, he went too far."

She stood there silent. "You know that your father left for the last time almost twenty years back but that's not entirely true. He came back again when you were four."

Charvi stood there frozen. "When I was four? Did mother know?" Marut shook his head.

"After he left, your house was searched many times but they didn't find anything. Then one night he came back. He handed me this and asked me to keep it safe. He said that the secret must be protected at all cost. The unworthy should not have it. He asked me to keep you safe as well for you can do what he could not. Then they found his tracks. I helped him escape and saw his shadow disappear in the mist for the last time before they could reach me or you and your mother."

Marut lowered his eyes in shame. "This time you found your father's secret, the ones I believe they were looking for, the ones chasing your father. So I took you to Rishi Bhavesh so that he could guide you. But he..." Marut stopped.

Then he looked at Charvi with pleading eyes. "But I never thought that it will come to this. I wanted to protect you; I wanted to keep you safe; Trinetra knows that I am speaking the truth. I didn't want you to follow his footsteps."

She felt the warmth of tears on her cheeks.

"You let him go?" she asked plainly. Old Marut closed his eyes, the shame was unbearable.

There was a dull thud, the noise of metal on wood. Marut jumped to his senses.

"Charvi we need to leave, now. I know that I have failed your parents but I loved them like my own. You are their child. Please don't make me fail you as well."

She looked away and gave a slow nod.

Marut quickly moved the almirah which revealed a small window. He helped her squeeze out of it and followed her. They landed in a small bush in the backyard. Her eyes fell on the broken backdoor hanging loosely from its hinges. The next thing, she felt the cool breeze in her hair and the drops of rain on her face. But it did not soothe her; her eyes only saw the road ahead frayed by the game of light and dark.

▼

Marut saw her from the distance. She sat there transfixed like a figure of wax in the pale Sun. The first hours of the dawn seemed the same like the dusk; the lingering light spoke many things. His old eyes had seen the follies of man yet he sat there looking at his staring at him in the eye.

"How is she doing?" asked a feminine voice. Marut smiled with difficulty.

"The past can be overbearing sometimes," he replied to Agrata, a fellow scholar.

"Yes, the past can haunt the present," she said. "But she has a good teacher. She will tide over it."

"You are too kind," was all Marut could manage.

"This string," said Marut. "My vow of celibacy is supposed to give me the strength to protect the ones who cannot and that is how I am to serve 'Trinetra'. Yet I fail in protecting the one I cared for most in this life."

"And Aranya knew that you loved him," she said giving his hand a squeeze.

"He trusted me Agrata, with his wealth, his secret and also with his family. Yet I failed there as well. I cannot let her go to Leu."

"Then go with her," she said. Marut looked at her surprised.

"There is an old saying, 'If the sparrow flies to distant heights then the sharp claws shall descend from heaven.' Her father never realized this. I cannot let her do the same," state Marut.

"And were you able to stop Aranya?"

Marut looked at her, a hint of anger flaring in them but then he dropped his gaze. Agrata took his hand in her's again.

"Maybe the old saying is true, yet maybe, maybe the little sparrow sees something from that high up, sees for the last time, which the other sparrows fail to comprehend."

He was staring at her smiling face, age had only made her sober. His old eyes were a bit moist and morning wind made him feel lighter. He gave a nod.

"Will I ever see you again?" he asked.

Agrata had a sad mile on her face.

"Whatever happens, you will find me waiting for you here or somewhere else."

Marut felt peace, that which his heart had yearned for.

The Chains of Old Bonds
(The Land of Rising Sun)

The pale morning was shrouded in mist and the little drops of rain did little to lighten Yani's spirits. He was asked many awkward questions after that dreadful night and had answered them the best he could. But the real answers eluded him as well.

He gave a sideways glance at his company, scores and scores of silent men in white rode beside him led by a man called Bodhan.

Yani closed his eyes, the silence was haunting.

"How far are we?" he asked though he knew the answer himself.

"Three bell hours," replied Bodhan.

"Alright." His eyes were fixed on the broad man, his face as expressionless as stone. He wanted to ask something, but hesitated.

"Can I ask you something?"

"Speak," came the reply.

"What did Agni do?"

The man cast him a glance. "It's not your concern," he spat back.

"Prince," added Yani. "You will refer to me as 'Prince' or 'Rajkumar'."

Bodhan had a mocking smile on his face. Yani shrugged.

"Whether you choose to tell me or not depends upon you, but you won't find Agni. He is the best tracker I know."

"We will," said Bodhan smiling.

"Let us see,"Yani smiled mockingly.

"You will be surprised to know as to who will help us in catching him," spoke Bodhan.

"Who?"

"The Raja of this Kingdom."

Yani was incredulous. "And why will he do that. Agni is his ward and a good friend of mine. My father loves him."

"It won't matter because…," Bodhan paused and trotted his horse closer to Yani's.

"Because we know a secret about him that you don't." The whispered words made him flinch. His vivid gaze was fixed on Bodhan's ruthless face.

▼

King Adhirath sat there still in his tall chair in the comfort of the feather pillows. The empty throne stared blankly at him as it shone in its lifeless beauty and splendour. The golden hall and its warmth made him shudder. The touch of grey in his charcoal black hair hinted at the onset of age, the secrets of old did what the vices of time could not. His gaunt face screamed of the uncertainty of the future and his searching eyes sought salvation. His eyes fell on the portrait of Amrita, his first wife. The memories came gushing. He was the young king and she, the beautiful daughter of Zamindar Ashwin. It was the festival of Jagoran (the festival of the first crop) when they first met, the season of abundance, the season of happiness. The pundit had prophesized that he would bear sons and riches of this world.

The lagna of the marriage was perfect. But the reality would have been never known by the false soothsayer. He had dreamt so many dreams then. The hall which was supposed to bear witness to the escalation of his line had screamed in silence for long. All his visions of the future had turned into unbridled imaginations.

There was a soft knock on the door.

"I asked you not to let anyone disturb me," spoke the grim King.

The door opened with a crack threatening the hinges to come loose. King Adhirath lifted his gaze. A large figure draped in saffron walked in followed by a few others.

"What is the meaning of this?"

"Father!" squeaked a voice.

"Son!" spoke the King in what was more than a whisper. Yani had a sad smile on his face, but King Adhirath kept staring.

"I dislike interfering in a father-son reunion, but I have business with you Raja."

The King shifted his eyes to the menacing man standing in his court with an accent of arrogance.

"First tell me who are you to throw questions in the hall of my father. And who gave you the authority to escort the crown prince?"

The man's face twisted into a crooked smile. He took a step forward.

"Do you believe that I have travelled thousands of paces to answer your questions?"

"How dare you!" roared Yani threateningly.

"At last the cub finds its tongue in his father's presence," smiled Bodhan.

"This is not Nisarga, Guru, remember that. You can lose more than your tongue here," threatened Yani again.

"And your father can lose all he has," replied Bodhan looking at the king. "After all, twenty years is a long time to hide a truth." There was an insidious smile on his face.

"Yani, to your room!" came Adhirath's voice. Yani was surprised.

"But father...."

"Now," cut in Adhirath. Bodhan was still smiling.

He gave a searching look to his father and then looked at Bodhan as he walked out slowly. The others closed the door behind him.

"What do you want?" asked Adhirath bluntly and Bodhan started laughing.

"Now you understand. Don't you, Raja?"

King Adhirath clenched his fists.

▼

"What happened, father? Why did you let that piece of garbage talk to you like that?" stormed Yani. King Adhirath sat on the throne, his hand on his forehead.

"Father...talk to me, please," entreated Yani after a moment.

"There is nothing to talk Yani; you should go and take some rest. These matters do not concern you."

"No," said Yani firmly.

"No?" reverberated the king.

"It does concern me. I saw Paksha and Agam die in front of my eyes. I don't know why. Then Sir Lonan accused you of conspiring against the kingdoms of the Land of the Setting Sun... the man you trusted...the man I..."

"What did you say?" interrupted Adhirath. Yani did not respond. "What did Lonan tell you, Yani?" Asked Adhirath sitting up straight.

Yani exhilarated. "That you have conspired against the Abode of the Seven by helping a man called Stranger and in due time you will be tried, your titles shall be stripped and your seat shall be taken." There was complete silence.

"Is it true, father?" asked Yani calmly.

"Go," replied the King.

But..."

"Go, now," shouted Adhirath. Yani turned around without another word and started walking. His mind was racing as he walked down the stairs. The answers to the question were haunting him and he knew that his father would never part with the secrets.

But then he paused. There was another who can answer his questions. 'Bodhan,' he whispered to himself.

▼

He stood outside the door, his eyes fixed on the exclusive woodwork.

"Rajkumar?" came Hiranya's voice. "Are you alright?"

Yani looked at him; he did not know how long he had been standing there. Like that.

"Shall I go with you?" asked the young captain. He was the replacement of Paksha and for that Yani felt a general resentment towards him.

"You are to do what you are told, stay here."

Yani turned around and knocked on the door.

"Come in," came a voice heavy with a northerner's accent.

He walked in and closed the door behind him.

"What do you want?" spoke the man casting him a glance. He seemed to be busy with something.

Yani hesitated for a moment.

"Speak boy. I don't have all day," chided the man. His arrogance was vile and made his hands itch.

Yani's brows were furrowed; it was not Nisarga yet the man in front of him was fearless.

"What do you want from my father?"

Bodhan turned around with a smile of curiosity on his face. "And why are you asking me this? What about your father?"

"I want answers from you," threatened Yani.

"And what if I don't answer you?"

He took a step closer, "This is not Nisarga. I can have your head with just the drop of a word."

Bodhan started to laugh. "You are not as intimidating as you may think of yourself to be. So get out while you still can. I am feeling rather merciful today and don't want to hurt little prince lings," he said and went back to his work.

"True, very true," smiled Yani. "But desperation can make a man intimidating."

Bodhan turned around. Yani slowly took out a knife from his pocket, a plain tilted kitchen knife.

"Now do you find me intimidating as seldom as an unarmed man does?" asked Yani with an inscrutable look on his face.

"How crude?" was Bodhan's smiling reply as he took a step towards Yani.

"Stay where you are or else I won't hesitate to use it. And you will answer my every question."

"Is that so?" asked Bodhan mockingly. "Have you ever used it before, Rajkumar? Other than at a westerner's fancy buffet, perhaps?"

Yani took a step back as Bodhan walked forward, his eyes wide with fear.

"Do you even know what it is to kill a man? To run a cold steel through someone's flesh as you see his life slowly slipping away, to feel the warmth of someone else's blood on your face, to have your hand stained for a lifetime. Do you?" Yani's hand trembled for a moment.

"I am warning you," he shouted, but Bodhan was onto him in a flash. He caught his hand and shook him like a rag doll. The knife fell on the floor. Then he pushed him which made him trip and fall.

When Yani looked up, Bodhan's tall frame was looming over him.

"The slum of Viratbhumi is the largest slum in the Land of the Rising Sun. There, one man kills another for a decent meal, some rice, meat and sura. I was born there, Rajkumar. I had more scars at your age than you have servants."

Then he hoisted him up by his collar. "The next time you raise a blade against me, I shall put it through your eye and I don't care whether you are a prince or not." Then he threw him away. "Now, get out."

Yani sat there on the floor, his head hung low. Bodhan could hear him crying.

"Tell me," he said looking up. "Tell me what I have to do? I want to know. I can't go on like this."

Bodhan's eyes were fixed on him, the flame of curiosity burnt brightly in them.

A Choice for a Choice
(The Land of the Rising Sun)

The stone danced on the water and then sank to the depths. Agni sat there silent, his eyes tracing the ripples in the pond.

"A very comfortable place to be," came a voice. Agni turned and saw Sidak. Param was not there.

"How did you find me?" He asked. Sidak was going to reply, "I don't want to know," he cut in and got back to what he was doing.

"Can I sit here?" asked the old Guru politely.

"Not my pond."

Sidak smiled and sat down beside him.

"Did you used to come here often? I mean before …."

"Yes, I find it peaceful here," replied Agni before he could finish.

"Hmm…it is a nice place to make memories."

"This place holds many …." paused Agni staring at the man. "This is where I met her when we were six." He put in bluntly.

"Malini, right. I have kept that in my mind," smiled Sidak. Agni could not help but smile.

"We never talked before properly, did we?" he asked.

Agni shook his head in disdain and looked away.

"All this running away can dull a man of his senses and rid him of his social skills."

"Abha," said Sidak.

Agni looked at him. "Who?"

"Her name was Abha, the girl I loved when I was young," replied the Guru.

"But, no offence, aren't gurus forbidden to marry?" asked Agni.

"But they aren't forbidden to love. No one has to take that away, not even the Gods."

Agni gave a smiling nod.

"I met her at my father's *kul* (house), our Gurukul, when we were eight. She aspired to be a Sikshacharika and I a Guru. We practically grew up together and fell in love with each other without even noticing."

Agni was staring at him.

"But time passed by like a flowing river and one day my father declared that it was time for her to leave."

"Then what happened?" asked Agni.

"She wanted me to forego my right of rebirth and give up my *dhaga*, the holy string. She wanted me to marry her."

"But you didn't?" cut in Agni.

Sidak shook his head. "I saw her leave. I saw the tears trickle down her cheeks."

Agni went silent. Sidak's face was gaunt.

"But you know what the funny thing is, Agni?" He looked at him.

"I have seen more than sixty years now," said Sidak. "And now I understand what I could not back then. I truly loved Abha but even if I had chosen her, then I wouldn't have been able to appreciate her, which I can now. I was too young to realize how much sacrifice my goals needed. But the truth is when the mind grows tired of thoughtfulness, the reality appears and real persons are better than memories."

"Where is she now?" asked Agni.

"Last I heard, she was the grandmother of two beautiful granddaughters at Viratbhumi," replied Sidak with a sad, yet meaningful smile on his face.

Agni dropped his gaze. Then he felt Sidak's hand on his shoulder.

"Don't even make the same mistake that I did. Like true love, true friends are also rare to come by and Vrish is one such."

He smiled in return. "I know Guruji. But there is another thing."

Sidak had a questioning look on his face.

"Didn't you say that real persons are better than memories?" asked Agni. "Well, he loves someone and I don't want it to turn into a memory like mine. He can have a new life, which I couldn't."

"That I why I did not chase after him even after realising my mistake of pushing him away."

Sidak gave a slow nod.

"I understand. You are a good man Agni and that is truly rare."

Agni smiled at that and said, "And I am sorry."

"Why is that?" asked Sidak with a questioning look on his face.

"It seems I misjudged you. I was losing my trust in you."

Sidak laughed at that. "People tend to do that often."

▼

Bani took the empty plates and handed them to Mahesh, the servant. The tavern was swarming with its regular brand of customers. There were shouts, screams asking for more sura and the cackle of gruff voices over pots.

'Nothing has changed,' thought Vrish and it brought a smile on his face as he looked on through the window like a thief. But still that huge figure with a pot of sura in his hand sitting in the far end of the eastern corner, was missing. It saddened his heart for a moment and then the final hours of that night came floating before his eyes. It filled him with bitterness.

He looked up again and saw the servants at their work. His eyes searched for Bani, but she had disappeared.

"Vrishji! Is that you?" came a voice. Vrish turned around startled.

The same beautiful face, plump, yet there was a soothing brightness to it. She stood there with an empty pot in her hand. Then she saw her approaching, she was saying something but his heart was beating too fast to listen. There was fear, anxiousness and yet the urge to go near her.

"I have been waiting so long but...," to Vrish's surprise, she slowly walked into his arms. His heart was beating fast. He couldn't help but wind her in his firm grip.

"I was so afraid...I heard a little of what happened at Nisarga but I knew you would come back." She looked up, her eyes red with tears. Vrish was staring at her helplessly.

But somewhere he felt peace, the lingering darkness slipped away slowly like tears of pain. Her words echoed in his ears, it removed the blindfold from his eyes.

Then she looked up staring at his happy face. "Where is Droh?" she asked. The sudden relief was gone and he kept on staring at her blankly.

▼

The palace of Himadri, looming at a distance in the dead of the night. A place which is home, a place which he knew brick by brick, every twig, every flower and even leaves. The faces that were in there did not belong to strangers, known or unknown, they had been there for a long time. The echoes of bondage yet screamed of peace while Agni's new world was a miasma of poisoned secrets.

"So, it leads us to that very place once again," said Sidak.

"My home," spoke Agni rather sarcastically.

"Home is where people are, home is where there are the ones you love," floated Vrish's voice to his ears. "And they shall always wait for you."

Agni was smiling. Then he turned around. "You came back?"

"I did," replied Vrish. "But that depends on what I am hoping to achieve."

Agni smiled. "And what is that?"

"To see whether it is the same man I called my brother or he doesn't care about that now," replied Vrish smiling.

"I always did care."

"I know. Sometimes it is hard to accept the facts of life; it is hard to come to the terms with the past to move on in the present."

Agni held his arms. "I am sorry, brother."

Vrish shook his head. "You need more time and so do I."

He was smiling.

"You did not tell her? Did you?" asked Agni.

Vrish shook his head gently. "No, I couldn't. I wasn't ready to accept the truth as well, whichever way it could have turned out to be. I just didn't realize that before."

Agni had a sad smile on his face.

"May be in the future, I will be. If I come back?" said Vrish.

Agni placed a hand on his shoulder and said reassuringly, despite his own gnawing fears, "That we will. Home is where there are the ones you love are and they shall wait for you."

Vrish smiled at his friend, the one he knew was still there, somewhere in all the darkness of the world.

Into the Palace of Lies
(The Land of the Rising Sun)

The lanterns hung from the post, the torches lighted up the pavements, their vague and uncanny reflections danced on the shallow pond. Two man-servants brushed away the evening sand off the marble floor as the bell tower announced the sixth hour of the moon.

"What's that foul stench?" said one of them, standing up straight.

"Go and see if the servant's bathroom is overflowing again," replied the elderly one.

"Why don't you go? My shift is coming to an end anyway. I don't want to end up cleaning before I go home."

"Well, I am not the one complaining," said the other with a smirk on his face.

"They think it's the wash room. We better move before they come this way," spoke Param in a hushed voice.

"Indeed and who wouldn't?" Agni smiled at the look on Sidak's face, his shaved head was glistening with muck.

The two servants didn't notice the four shadows gliding past the pillars. They paused in front of the door between the servant's quarters and royal house.

Vrish took out a pin and got himself busy picking the lock.

"What's taking so long?" whispered Agni angrily.

"Almost done," replied Vrish, irritated.

"Hurry, the guards can come any moment."

"Almost, almost….Done!" said Vrish exuberantly but there was no reply.

He turned around and saw that Agni was staring at something. He shifted his gaze and saw a young guard standing there. His face half open and the untied waist belt in one hand as he walked out of the washroom.

He recognized him as Kanti, a young recruit. They had run into each other quite a number of times.

"Agniji, Vrishji," he mumbled and when it became obvious he went for his sword.

"Stop," warned Agni. "Don't be foolish Kanti."

The boy was shaking, yet his hand was on the hilt of the blade.

"I cannot let you all go in."

"I don't see any other choice," replied Vrish.

"I took an oath to protect Rajaji," said the fifteen-year-old.

"And we don't mean him any harm," said Agni.

Kanti saw Param's hand on the hilt of his dagger. He looked at Sidak, his eyes were wide. "I do not trust you," replied Kanti.

Then something happened. Agni heard footsteps and at a distance saw an old servant passing by. Kanti saw it as well. He glanced at Agni and then was about to shout. But Param gagged him and drew out his dagger.

"No, wait," shouted Vrish but by that time it was over.

Agni stood there stunned. The boy collapsed on the floor choking in his own blood. Agni saw his eyes, pleading and young as tears trickled out of them. He saw his life slip away.

Vrish looked away, hiding his face. Then he drew out his own sword in rage and pointed at Param.

"He was fifteen," he shouted as Param stood there like a stone. Agni was only staring at Sidak.

"He did what he had to, Agni! Param is not a killer. And we don't have time."

"Vrish please," said Agni, not looking at his friend.

"What?" asked Vrish astounded.

"Lower your weapon," he said. "Please". Sidak gave a nod as he walked in followed by Param.

Vrish stood there, his gaze transfixed on his friend.

"Why?" he asked but Agni remained silent. He did not answer his question. But he did not face his friend either. There was something stirring inside him which he couldn't explain, not to Vrish.

▼

The loud knock on the door startled King Adhirath.

"Come in," he slurred.

Captain Hiranya walked in and gave a bow; for a moment his eyes fell on the half empty pitcher of 'sura'.

"Why are you here at this hour, Captain? As I remember I did not ask for you," slurred the King.

"No Maharaj, but I bring grave tidings. A guard was found murdered in the servant's quarters. We have locked all doors. I believe the intruders are still inside the castle, so I have come to lead you to your room."

"What? You fool?" shouted the King as he stood up. "Get up on your feet fast and fetch my son. I want him here right now."

Captain Hiranya stood up quickly. "Yes, Maharaj."

"Where is Dhanvin? I want him here too and you search the castle. I want those men found and brought before me within a bell hour."

"The Maharaja's wish is my command," came a hoarse voice as the door banged open.

Agni walked in followed by the others.

King Adhirath froze for the moment but then his expression changed.

"How did you get past the guards?" roared the captain's voice as he took out his blade in a flash.

Agni did not reply, his gaze was transfixed on the king.

"Hiranya, leave us," said the King calmly. "Go to my son and keep him in his room until I send word."

"But Maharaj…"

"Now," barked the king.

They waited for the Captain to leave as King Adhirath poured himself another glass.

He downed it at one go and then looked at Agni.

"From the look of things, I can say that you are not here to harm me."

"You know why I am here. If you had been unsure then I believe you wouldn't have sent your captain away for cowards seldom depend on others," replied Agni.

"Coward?" asked the King smiling.

"I have not heard of brave men killing innocents to hide their…," paused Agni.

"Incapabilities." Agni saw Adhirath tighten his grip around the glass. Then he calmed himself.

"And which brave men do you speak of? Solon, the very man who plotted all this or your father, who left you in my hands and fled."

"At least he chose to die to save his son. Would you have done the same for Yani Adhirathji?" asked Agni smiling.

"Yani is precious to me," the King spat.

"Sadly a fact he is unaware of."

The King smiled, shaking his head.

"One loss, one single loss and it has driven you to madness. Was she that important to you? What a pitiful death for someone so important?" sighed the King in mockery.

Agni could feel his blood surging but he felt Vrish's hand on his shoulders.

"She was beautiful even in her death and you not even in your life," replied Agni from his deep wrenching sorrow.

The King gave a nod. "May be so but there is no beauty in death Agni, believe me. The ones who are gone are gone."

Agni felt his fingers twitching.

"But that is my thought. I believe that a living person's life is more important than a dead girl's. Your quest, whatever it is, will only end in failure and the losses will keep piling." King Adhirath sat down and continued, "I am a king, Agni. Himadri might be a small kingdom but yet I am more powerful than many in this entire land. I can give you a peaceful life, away from all this. Isn't that what your father wanted?"

"I am only here for that which belongs to me," Agni was seething with repressed anger.

King Adhirath slowly shook his head. "I took you for a smarter man, Agni. But tell me, you found your way in but how do you propose to escape?"

"I do not need to. You will show me the way out and also give us four horses," replied Agni.

"And why should I?"

"We know everything Adhirath," replied Vrish hoarsely.

The King started to laugh. "And who will believe you four? Two murderers, a vagabond guru and his disciple."

"Questions Adhirathji, questions. The very thing that drives a man either to his destiny or his doom and Yani is very fond of them," replied Agni smiling.

"But he will seek proof and in absence of that he will fall silent," spat back Adhirath.

"Well, we can arrange that," spoke Sidak at last. "Three maids and one Vaidya, the ones you have sent away to Nisk. The ones who were there that very day when the Rajkumar was supposed to be born. "

King Adhirath was stunned. Agni saw fear in his eyes. Sidak was smiling.

"How do you know all this?" he asked petrified.

"Your house is as honest as you are Raja," replied Sidak with that persisting smile. "And even if you do not let us reach Yani, I have ways of reaching others who will be more interested in your affairs with Solon. The Abode is unforgiving. I think that even a few in your kingdom as well will be eager to hear our tale."

King Adhirath was fuming, his rage clear on his face. "You all," he said pointing at them. "You all have been my guest for twenty long years. This is how you repay me for my hospitality, for the salt and rice, for your coffers that my gold has filled?"

"The price you have taken for that is too high. If it were up to me, I would not have given you the chance to speak a single word," spoke Vrish with malice.

King Adhirath fell silent but he was breathing heavily.

"The letter," said Agni firmly.

The King stood up slowly and walked to the back of the throne. He came back with a letter in his hand. Agni snatched it from his hand and shoved it inside his pocket.

"It was a cursed day when I took you in, Agni. Your father was branded a traitor and you prove it true as his blood runs through your veins," rebuked the King.

"I pity you, you are truly an incapable man. I was always loyal to you and yet you failed to preserve that. You even chided away the son who could have been yours. Maybe that is why Trinetra never saw fit to grant you the boon of creation." Agni was beyond civilities with this man.

"You insolent bastard," shouted the King and raised his hand. But he stopped short as felt the touch of cold steel on his neck.

"You killed my family. Don't give me the opportunity to return the favour," whispered Vrish.

The King lowered his hand as they made their way towards the door.

"I was going to feel sorry for you Agni," spoke Adhirath with contempt. "But now I shall enjoy seeing your fate."

Agni did not understand the meaning of his words but his eyes were fixed on him as the door closed slowly.

▼

Agni and the others walked out of the door and took a sharp left.

"We make our ways towards the South gate," said Agni as he led them on.

"They are there," shouted one of the guards.

"Run," said Sidak and they rushed towards the door. But the door opened by itself and on the other side stood a battalion of thirty strong archers.

"The traitor threatened the Maharaj, notch," shouted the Captain.

"Stop," came a roaring voice. "The Maharaja wishes for them to leave, unharmed."

Agni turned and saw Dhanvin, the new general of the armed forces.

The archers lowered their arrows.

"Leave, traitor, and never come back. Take your horses and go."

They were allowed to pass. The palace gate was open for them as the guards eyed him with hatred and the servants lowered their gaze. Agni's heart was pounding.

'Murderers,' screamed someone and Agni's heart skipped a beat.

He looked back and saw many faceless shadows.

'It was I who was wronged,' he wanted to scream but he knew that there were no ears which would listen.

They trotted out of the palace gate and it was shut behind them. Agni glanced back once; he knew he would never step in there again, ever again. The people who knew him shall remember him as someone else from now on.

"We ride hard till dawn until we reach the cover of the forest," said Sidak. They were already near the broad roads.

Agni was about to say something when he saw an arrow whirl past him. He looked back.

"Riders," shouted Param and they increased their speed. The four horses galloped through the night. Agni glanced back and saw at least twenty of them, draped in white.

"These are not Adhirathji's men," said Agni looking at Sidak.

"Nimit," the word floated to his ears over the wind.

"Damn you Adhirath," cursed Vrish.

'I was going to feel sorry for you Agni,' the words echoed in his ears.

"He didn't want us killed in his palace, he didn't want to stain his hands," said Sidak.

"That is why he gave us the scroll, that scheming bastard," cursed Vrish.

"They are gaining," shouted Param from the back. Then he saw Vrish's horse slowing down and his eyes fell on the blood trickling down its thighs. The horse was hit and it was a matter of time before it would collapse. Two on one horse wouldn't make it. Agni looked at Vrish and saw fear in his eyes.

"Ride ahead, we will slow them down," came Sidak's voice.

Then suddenly their horses screeched to a halt as a black rider jumped in front of them out of nowhere. The man was all draped in black. "Get out of the way," threatened Agni.

"Follow me if you want to live," said the man and turned his horse around.

He disappeared into the valley.

Agni looked at Vrish. There was no time to decide.

"Your horse," he said simply. Vrish also gave a nod. The two horses rushed into the darkness.

"Agni," came Sidak's faint call from a distance as they took the bend.

They saw the vague figure of the man ahead as he took turns and bends into the maze of alleys. The road became darker and the houses thicker in number.

"This way," came the rider's voice and he led them into a backside stable behind some inn. They came to a halt. Sidak and Param had caught up.

"What happened?" asked Sidak as he stopped beside Agni. He simply pointed his finger at the hooded in reply.

The man came down from his horse and closed the stable gate but Agni and others remained mounted.

"Who are you? And why have you led us here?" asked Agni but the man stood there silent like a puppet.

"It was I who asked Hiranya to bring you here," came a second voice as another hooded man appeared from the shadows. He pulled down his hood.

"How are you Agni?" asked Yani, a sad smile lingering on his face.

The Ashes of what was Once Home
(The Land of the Setting Sun)

Vrish and others sat at a distance while Agni stood with Yani. Vrish made sure that he did not even glance at the Rajkumar once.

"He is still upset with me, isn't he?" asked Yani.

"He is upset because of a lot of things; you are not a particular reason," replied Agni.

"True, any man will feel like that if he loses his entire family."

Agni did not reply, he had lost something precious as well, but Yani did not know.

"Why have you brought us here, Yani? If it's about Nisarga then you must know that I cannot tell you anything," said Agni.

"Why Agni? Why can't you tell me? My father won't tell me, and those people at Nisarga didn't say anything. Don't you understand Agni," he took a step closer. "I saw people die in front of me. The ones I knew, I cared for."

Agni was shaking his head with a wry smile on his face. "I promised your father. I promised him that I won't tell you anything in exchange of something, and unlike him, I don't break promises."

"Is this about the fire at the docks?" asked Yani bluntly.

Agni paused. "Did he do it?" Yani asked again, his face dark.

"It is better that you don't get mixed into all this," replied Agni after a brief pause.

"But I want to know," Yani almost shouted and the others looked at them.

"Is everything fine Agni," came Vrish's voice.

"Yes", said Agni but he saw Vrish's gaze lingering on for a moment.

"I am sorry for shouting," Yani apologized quickly. Then he held Agni's hand.

"Please Agni, these people, the ones that are chasing you, they won't stop at anything and they also hold father in some kind of a bargain which I believe won't turn out to be good."

Agni felt pity for Yani. Even after being treated the way he was by his father, he still cared for him. He placed a hand on his shoulder. "It will all be over soon. They will give up once the word reaches them."

"No they won't, Agni," blurted out Yani. "This man Bodhan, he is a fiend. He won't stop at anything and he will never let us go."

Agni smiled. "He will, once he doesn't have anything to chase. He will quit,"

Yani's eyes became wide. "You are leaving? You are leaving the Land of the Rising Sun?"

Agni gave a slow nod. "I hope that solves your problems."

"No," said Yani as he caught hold of him by his shoulders. "I don't want you to leave. We can sort this out."

"There is no other choice," replied Agni. Yani was staring in his blue eyes, his face was gaunt, unshaved and ruthless, yet he saw his old friend somewhere in there.

"How did it all come to this?" said Yani with pleading eyes.

"One man said something five hundred years ago which he shouldn't have," replied Agni sarcastically.

"Darshana?" asked Yani surprised.

"Don't go groping in the dark. Get back to your life, my friend. Find a girl and settle down," advised Agni.

"And you? What about you?"

Agni climbed his horse and the others followed suit. "Farewell Yani! Go home and be happy. You have a good life; don't waste it."

"Is there anything I can do for you?" asked Yani desperately.

"Be a better king than your father," replied Agni.

The next moment, dust flew in the air as the four of them raced into the darkness of the night led by Hiranya who was to lead them outside the city walls to safety.

Yani stood there staring. "Take care my friend. Rest assured, we will meet again." He had half a smile on his face.

▼

The cracking sound startled the armed preachers outside Bodhan's room but they passed by in silence as their faces turned frigid again.

"Foolish Raja," Bodhan fumed, "I should have caught him when I had the chance instead of listening to that bastard." He cursed himself in solitude.

There was a soft knock on the door.

"Be gone," roared Bodhan.

This time the door opened and Yani walked in slowly.

"What do you want? I am not in the mood to suffer your stupidity."

Yani cribbed. "Alright, but you may want to hear this."

"Unless you can conjure that sneaky bastard, I do not have anything to do with you."

"I am no mage," said Yani as he closed the door. "But you will regret later if you do not hear me out."

Yani picked up Bodhan's cask from his desk. His eyes saw the broken shards.

"Such a shame, those were fine glasses," he said and drank straight.

"I do not have the time boy; I shall say this one more time. Speak or be gone."

"It is true, time is what you don't have," replied Yani smiling.

Bodhan caught him by his throat.

"Don't mock me boy, don't you dare mock me," he hissed. "If it was not for your foolish father, I could have had him by now and also the prophecy."

"Darshana's prophecy?" asked Yani with a crooked smile on his face.

Bodhan let him go. "How do you know that?"

"Don't be alarmed," spoke Yani brushing the dirt off his vest. "I have no interest in your prophecy. I only want to know as to why my father is helping you and in return I shall disclose Agni's plan to you."

"What plan?"

"Where Agni intends to go from here?"

"And how do you know this? I was there all along and you weren't," said Bodhan with suspicion.

"I have my ways and are you interested in learning the secret or the measures of obtaining it?" asked Yani pompously. "Hiranya found out from Dhanvin who overheard them as they left," he lied.

"And how do I know you are not lying?" Bodhan was not impressed.

"You will know, that is the first thing you will," replied Yani.

"Your palace won't be able to hide you Rajkumar if I learn that your information is incorrect or you are leading me away from him."

Yani clenched his fists. "I will not take any more of your insults. We had a deal."

"Speak," said Bodhan smiling. Yani took a deep breath, "He is planning on leaving the Land of the Rising Sun and he was heading south after he left Himadri." It was Hiranya who had escorted them out of the south gate on their request; he had returned and informed him of their choice.

Bodhan was astounded. "Are you sure?" he asked.

"Quite certain."

"South you say, and then there is only one way," spoke Bodhan more to himself. He hurried to get his robes.

"And now it's your turn," said Yani.

Bodhan cast him a smiling glance and chortled.

"You are one adamant boy. But you will not believe it if you hear it from me."

"That was not the deal," said Yani with gritted teeth.

"Don't worry Rajkumar, I am a warrior and I do not go back on my word. You will hear the truth from someone who will not leave a shred of doubt in your mind."

"Who?" asked Yani.

"Your father," replied Bodhan with a savage smile on his face.

▼

The morning sang a sweet note as the crisp rays of the sun danced on the curves and the ledges of Himadri.

"How dare you accuse me? I lost the letter because of your incompetence. I gave you the best chance and yet you failed," raged King Adhirath.

"Be careful of your words Raja, I am not one of your subjects," replied Bodhan sharply.

"Yet you stand in my chamber, in my palace and in my kingdom. This is not Nisarga, this is Himadri and I am the Raja. You will know your place," warned Adhirath.

"Oh, and what about your successor?" asked Bodhan smiling.

"You are bound by oath, sworn to silence that you shall not speak of this to anyone after I help you," snarled the king.

"You do not have to teach me the old ways, Raja. I am a warrior and a guru, my word is steel. But tell me, if you are such a pious man, then how can you break the most ancient of traditions?"

"How dare you," fumed the King. "Yani is my son, mine. Even Rishi Vajra didn't follow that path. Two of his sons were not his blood and yet they proved themselves to be more than any of his true blooded heirs. Who cares whom Yani belonged to? He will remain my son as long as he lives."

Bodhan was smiling.

"You shall not take my son from me and you will keep your word," threatened the king.

Bodhan gave a curt bow. "That I will and you shall respond to my call as well if such a time comes. Do not forget that," he said and started for the door.

The king stood there glaring, the deep seeded hatred burning in his heart. He despised that man from his core.

Bodhan disappeared round the bend and stood in front of Yani behind the wood work. He sat there, his head between his knees and Bodhan's massive figure towering over him.

"I hope that answers your queries. The deal is done," he spoke laxly. Yani looked up.

"I am not his son?" The words fell out of his mouth.

"I am sworn to silence," replied Bodhan with a mocking smile.

"Then who am I?" The tears rolled out his cheeks.

Bodhan looked on with disgust. "Life is never fair, everyone should know that," were his parting words.

▼

The great sea had a rhythm of its own. The waves crashed on the rocks and sprayed salt water on the careless passersby. The gulls cawed and croaked and many took to the air as came the call of home. Only a few sat there by the vastness and stared on aimlessly; not everyone was so lucky to have a home.

The setting sun turned the water into a lake of orange nectar in the heart of the stretch of salt water. Yani closed his eyes as the sound of hooves on sand drew nearer.

"There you are, Rajkumar!" said Hiranya as he jumped down. "We have been looking everywhere for you. Rajaji is very worried."

Yani remained silent.

"Is everything alright?"

Yani looked at him after a brief pause and it didn't escape Hiranya's eyes that something was amiss.

"Can I ask you something, Hiranya?"

"Of course Rajkumar," replied the man quickly.

"What binds you to Himadri? Is it duty or blood?"

Hiranya was a bit taken aback but after his gaze lingered on Yani, he smiled.

"Can I have a seat?" he asked and Yani slowly nodded.

"Is this question coming from the rajkumar of the kingdom I serve or a common man?"

Yani felt amused. "A friend," he replied.

"Then the answer is neither. Blood does not bind me here because my family is at the village of Jaldhar and my notion of duty is different from others. It's progress. I want to live my life on my own terms," said Hiranya.

Yani was surprised.

"Don't be surprised Rajkumar. However queer it may sound for a soldier to say that he is not bound by duty, it is the truth. I have come to love my job only because of the fact that I can be someone. If I gain honour on that path as well then it is an added boon," he smiled.

"That means gold or power can sway your loyalty?" asked Yani.

"I never said that. If gold was the answer, then I would have been a mercenary, and as for power, nobody wants a dog which easily changes masters. They are either killed or cast away when their need is over."

"So you are honour-bound because the consequences of treachery can be fatal?" asked Yani.

"Aren't we all, Rajkumar? Every man has a beast inside him and it resents control. But if we let it have its way, then the world will burn. On the other hand, I cannot cast it away from my depths, then I would have become a saint," replied Hiranya smiling.

Yani started laughing.

"I hope my answers did not offend you?" he asked.

"I like an honest and ruthless man more than a jackal wearing a sheep's clothing," replied Yani smiling.

Then he stood up. "Hiranya, you want to rise and I want something which I can call my own. I think I can find a way for both of us."

Hiranya looked on confused. "See, I have something to do, rather right a wrong, and for that I need help."

"I will do what you command, you are the Rajkumar of Himadri," replied Hiranya diligently. Yani shook his head.

"It's not like that. This path can be difficult but if I succeed then I will reach new heights and you can never speak of this to anyone. So I will need someone I can trust and so there lies my proposition," paused Yani.

"You will swear your sword to me and only me. Your duty to me shall come first." Hiranya kept looking at him blankly. "Even before Maharaj, my father."

Hiranya sat there silent.

"It is for the good of Himadri for I am Himadri; or that I shall be, a king is his kingdom and its subjects," added Yani.

Hiranya gave a slow nod. Yani was pleased.

"Good, now before we start, tell me this. If you were a wanted man, wanted to leave the Land of the Rising Sun and you were heading south, then what would have been the safest way?"

The South Wind
(The Land of the Rising Sun)

A gni sat by the rippling cascades of Sheetaldhara, the letter clutched in his hand. His heart beat frantically. The melody of the streaming water filled his ears and he closed his eyes.

"There you are!" said Vrish as he sat down beside him. Then he saw the letter in his hand.

"You haven't opened it, have you?"

Agni slowly shook his head.

"Well I would have taken my time as well if I were in your shoes," said Vrish.

"It's not that Vrish." Vrish looked at Agni. "It's just that... I don't know what to do anymore."

"Neither do I," smiled Vrish. "We are with ruthless people and there are ruthless people chasing us," said Vrish sarcastically.

"And I don't know how to change that," replied Agni. "This road," he continued. "I don't know where it will lead me."

"Then you should decide first, my friend," said Vrish.

Agni was staring at him. "I want to find her," replied Agni. "If she is alive."

"Then you should open that," pointed Vrish. "If my mother would have been alive out there somewhere, then I would have done the same."

Agni looked at the envelope in his hand. The broken seal of Old Giana gleamed a bit. He looked at Vrish and gave a slight nod. He opened the letter slowly; the paper was thin with words inscribed on it in green ink. It was almost magical. There was a thin journal inside as well but Agni opened the letter first.

"Dear Solon,
When you will read this, it is most likely that I shall not be a part of this realm, but knowing that my son is in your hands, I shall find peace.

I did not share many things with you in the recent past and yet you have followed each of my word without question. That shows your love for me, for which I am sincerely grateful. I am sorry things have turned out the way they have for it was never my choice.

The world of Gaya is shrouded in a mist, an undying way of beliefs cloud our minds. It has to come to an end but whether my son will walk that path or not, a choice I leave to him and you, as his guardian. But to make such a choice you must see what I have seen. The Sage shall help you if you follow such a course and so will many others in disguise, some as gurus and some as saints. You already know where to find Sage and even if you do not find him, he most certainly will. But the truth must remain with you except the ones who already know. King Adhirath will be reluctant, but the son I gave him shall aid you as the chosen secret to mould a man like Adhirath. This secret is the only way to reach the scepter of Lord Kubha which is the other part of the key I gave you.

Lastly, I shall say one thing for the son whom I will never see grow, name him well and find his mother, my

Serene, for you shall find more than one reason. If you can pursue my son to lead a normal and happy life after showing him the truth, then like any selfish father, I shall know that you have done your friend a great service.

> Your brother, your King.
> Son of Lord Xavier, Eighth in line
> King of Athena and lastly one of
> the pack of four.
> King Arkansas

"He always used to call me by that name, 'The Sage'," came Sidak's voice. He had a sad smile on his face as Agni looked at him, his eyes red with tears of blood, and his lips quivering.

"Her name is Serene, my mother?"

Sidak gave a slow nod. "I have heard that name many times from your father. He loved her a lot."

Agni let go of the letter and covered his eyes. Sidak was the one to pick it up before Vrish. Then Agni walked away without saying a word to Vrish.

"I have to go," said Agni. "I have to find her. I have to find my mother."

"Agni," came Sidak's voice. "I don't know whether I should be telling you this now."

Agni looked back and saw Sidak standing with the letter in one hand and the scroll in another. "Somehow," said Sidak, "your father's handwriting matches with that of the last sentence of the scroll, 'I hide the secret where my soul is at peace'."

▼

The morning Sun was peeking from the horizon; the red tongue licked the grey heavens and lifted the city from its slumber.

"Rajkumar was supposed to be here by now," spoke Hiranya more to himself.

"Don't hold your breath, he is always late," smirked one of the guards standing beside him.

Yani had ordered him to assemble six of the finest archers in Himadri; they were to head towards Nada.

The first bell rang and the palace door opened. Yani walked out dressed in leather and mail.

Hiranya gave the guard a glance and approached the Prince.

"Your carriage is ready Rajkumar," he declared with a salute.

"I won't take the carriage. Find me the swiftest horse; I will ride," ordered Yani.

"But the road is too long."

Yani smiled at his champion. "Do as you are told, my friend, it will save us precious time."

Hiranya gave a reluctant nod and scurried of to the stable followed by the others while Yani stood there in the Sun and closed his eyes. The night before came trickling back to him. He had asked for King Adhirath's permission to travel to Nada for a reason he did not state.

"This is not the time to fool around. There is trouble brewing and Himadri needs its Rajkumar," was the King's reply.

Then he had announced his intention of leaving Himadri whether the King liked it or not. It was the first time he had stopped the man from laying a hand on him.

"Your mount is ready," came Hiranya's voice and Yani opened his eyes.

He gave one last glance at the Palace as he climbed his horse. It seemed like a lifeless edifice to him.

"Ride," he commanded and kicked his horse and the palace started to disappear behind them.

"It is not my place to ask but Rajaji did not come to bid you farewell?" asked Hiranya.

"The reason of my travel did not please him," smiled Yani.

"Why are we going to Nada in the first place?"

"No more questions Hiranya, it is not the time," was the Rajkumar's brazen reply.

Hiranya fell silent immediately.

'It is true that when one knows his roots, the world seems to be a less threatening place,' Yani thought. "A day shall come when the prince shall becomes king," he mouthed the words in silence as his eyes fell on Guru Bhas' letter in his hand which he had received that morning. It held clues as to what Agni was looking for and a few tales of Nimit.

▼

It has already been fourteen days since they had left Himadri. They had taken the longer way through the forest of Kyat, crossing Anu rather than the high road on the eastern bank of Sheetaldhara. It would have taken them half the time to reach Nada, but the longer way was safer.

"I still do not understand as to why would Agni's father steal the scroll in the first place and then hide it again?" asked Vrish.

Agni sat by the fire peering over the notes on the city of Nisarga, Lord Kubha and King Adhirath that his father had left for Solon along with the letter. Their camp in the wetlands was a few bell hours' journey from Nada. Sidak was against entering the city at night as it would draw suspicion. Dawn was almost near as Param moved on to put out the fire removing the traces of the camp.

Agni put the letter back in his knapsack.

"Agni! What do you think? Why would he do that?" asked Vrish again.

"Remember when we used to play *kanamachi* (hide and seek) as children?" asked Agni.

"Yes, I do, but what does that have to do with anything?" he asked bewildered.

"Suppose if one of the hider gives away the position of another to the seeker and the second hider comes to know of that, what will happen then?" asked Agni.

Vrish scratched his head. Sidak was smiling as he listened to the conversation.

"The hider will change spots, I suppose," replied Vrish.

"That is what has happened. Solon told me before his death that my father was betrayed and that is why he couldn't come to the Land of the Rising Sun with me. From his letter it is certain that he knew....." paused Agni, 'his impending doom,' were the words he wanted to say but couldn't bring himself to that.

"But Agni, from what I read in the letter, your father already knew that he was going to die. If he knew he was going to be betrayed, then why didn't he do something about it?" argued Vrish.

Agni remained silent. That part has eluded him also; it didn't make sense, just as Vrish had said.

"Perhaps he did not get the time to act; maybe the word reached him too late," cut in Sidak.

"Maybe he had the time but the word came in through a source which he didn't trust completely. It could have been affirmed by another reliable source, that is King Crixus, and this letter was a half measure in case the worst came true," replied Agni.

Sidak gave a sigh. "You could be right, Agni. Sadly, we don't have a way of confirming these theories. It is only King Crixus who can shed some light on this matter."

Agni felt the first rays of the sun and the slight warmth as the sky lit up slowly.

"Finally," said Vrish as he stood up. The pale light penetrated the blanket of darkness and its thin rays fell on 'the City of Scavengers'. The 'Sheetaldhara' moved in its slow pace and met the Sea, on the convocation sat the lawless city.

The rugged buildings gutted by time bared its fangs at the onlookers. The ships that ventured upriver towards the dry docks were visible even from that distance.

"One of those shall bear us west," said Vrish.

"Then what are we waiting for," said Agni as he stood up.

The new dawn brought in new hopes.

▼

The city was quite different from Himadri. The streets were narrow with shanties and bunk houses, the open drains stank of foul water. The guards sat around chatting and smoking. The children were playing on the streets dodging carts and palanquins and the women went around with morning chores. One of the guards haggled a shopkeeper for a bribe. Agni sat there stunned.

"Nada has always been like this; this is a tainted city." Sidak smiled and said.

"That explains why the guards didn't ask for a permit even once," replied Vrish instead.

"Isn't this the most prosperous port of the South?" asked Agni.

"Rich, yes, but I won't use the term prosperous. See, Nada is ruled by Kabala, the pirate son of Maharaj Shambhu. Back then,

Anu, Nada and Nisk were but the three cities of one kingdom, Agnikund. But after Maharaja Shambhu's death, the three cities were split amongst the three brothers. Anu was taken by the benevolent one, Nisk by the enterprising one and last Nada was claimed by the notorious one," Sidak explained.

"That explains it all," Agni smiled looking at the condition of the city around him.

"Well there is a story behind that as well," said Sidak. "It is rumoured that Kabala had an eye on one of the wives of his eldest brother. So he was cast away with the worst share to teach him a lesson. Back then, Nada was nothing but a few shanties. Kabala's myriad ways and unconcerned views of law made it flourish in a different way. It ate into Anu's trade and thus turned into a port city of great promise."

"Well, we must thank our stars that it happened the way it did. If Kabala had been a perfect brother, then we would have had bigger problems," stated Vrish.

"Someone's doom's day is someone's dream's day, the balance never tilts," said Sidak and all of them laughed.

"After we find an inn to stay, we better head towards the docks," said Agni.

"Yes, but carry your gold with you. Nada is not famous for its attendants," warned Sidak.

"Well, there is one," pointed Vrish at a run-down structure, albeit with a large crowd in front of it.

"I think we better come back sometime later," said Agni.

"No, it's a local matter. They leave the outsiders alone if they don't interfere," came the voice of an elderly man.

All of them turned around to look at the man. "You are travellers, I take?" he asked.

"Yes," replied Agni.

"You looking to spend the night somewhere?" he asked.

"Let us get to that inn Agni," Vrish whispered in Agni's ears.

"Actually I own that inn," said the man with a buck-toothed grin.

"Then what are you doing out here?" blurted out Vrish.

"And who says that the inn-keeper doesn't have the right to enjoy a drink in the Sun?"

"Things are different here, Vrish," spoke Sidak in a hushed voice but Vrish paid no heed.

"Aye, you can say that again. Now I don't like to talk much, do you folks want a room for the night or not?"

"How much?" asked Agni.

"Three ginis and you get my best, two you get the worst and one, you sleep with the horses."

Agni tossed him four. "Take care of the horses," he said.

"Certainly, not much horses here to take care of anyway," he chuckled.

They came down from their horses as the man led them inside. A scene was unfolding a few steps away from the door. Agni saw a man being beaten with a stick by an old woman and being kicked by others; a young woman lay unconscious a few steps away from them.

"What's happening here?" he asked.

"The same," replied the inn-keeper. "That man Kush, he is a bloody drunken sod and wife beater too. This time he went too far and she ain't moving. So her mother and relatives came here to give him his just due. By the way, my name is Banshi, and if you need anything, just stick your head out. Remember that, I won't be telling that twice."

Agni stood there staring at the young woman. She was fair to look at, it numbed his senses to think how a man could treat his wife like that.

Then suddenly, Agni saw everything turn grey and the noises around him became barely audible. There was a woman who lay unconscious on the green grass and a child sat beside her crying in the open field. Another woman came and caught hold of his arm and dragged the child along. "Mother," cried the child but the woman did not stop.

"Leave him alone," shouted Agni and the world reshaped itself around him into reality. Everyone turned their heads and the old woman stopped.

"What did he say?" barked one of them.

"The lad is just dazed from the sun, been talking to himself for a while. Not right in the head, Kashi. Nothing for you to worry about." explained Banshi politely.

"Then pour some water in his bloody mouth or I will do it for him."

"Aye," said Banshi. "Come along now, to the bed with you." He almost dragged Agni inside.

Vrish helped Agni lie down on the bed.

"You should be careful out there," said Banshi. "They are not nice people. It was your dumb luck that I was there. Dumb luck, get it?" he snorted.

Vrish threw him a gini. "Get the fuck out of here." The man fell silent.

"Make yourself comfortable and call out if you need anything," said Banshi peevishly. 'Trinetra knows why I always get the weird folks,' he grumbled on his way out.

"What happened out there, Agni?" asked Vrish as Param closed the door.

"I don't know," he mumbled. "My head hurts."

"Get some rest," said a concerned Vrish and Agni closed his eyes.

A little steam was rising from the scabbard of the black blade and it did not escape Siak's eyes.

▼

Yani walked up the stone stairs of the wooden palace. The walls were adorned with ancient scriptures and gold statues of saints sat on small podiums. He paused wondering what these statues meant, for what he knew about Kabala, he could barely be called a learned man.

"These are only for decorations lad," came a gruff voice laced with a southerner's accent.

"Indeed," replied Yani.

"Indeed?" asked the man.

"For what I know of Raja Kabala, he doesn't have interest in these things," replied Yani.

The man stroked his moustache, his shaven cheeks glistened with oil and a strong perfume surrounded him like an aura. His eyes were shining black with some *surma* marking the edges.

"How much more do you know about Raja Kabala?" asked the man with an inquisitive smile.

"Well he is pirate king to be put in bluntly," replied yani. "But first tell me who are you?"

"My name is Kendra Shambhunath, I am a captain by rank and Raja Kabala's best man," replied the man with a flimsy bow.

"My name is Yani. I am the Rajkumar of Himadri and I have no more titles to give," smiled Yani.

The man laughed out aloud. "Truth gives a man more titles than one can take," he said. "Come, let me take you to the throne room."

"So you never answered my question. How much do you know about the king?" he said as he led Yani up the stairs.

"Well, he has a good taste for one, which I can already see." The man chortled and Yani continued, "From what I have heard, he has a lust for gold; he is fond of dice games and has an eye for women. Though history says that he shouldn't have cast them in a few places."

The man guffawed at his words. "That's true."

"And also, he is man of sword. But I also believe not every man knows how to wield a sword, and every swordsman is not as smart and learned as a few others. A time may come when one outshines the other, but the two of them together can outshine many."

The man gave a nod. "Very smart, that's very smart for someone of your age."

"That I am, Shambhunath. Or shall I say Raja Kabala, son of Maharaja Shambhu of the house of Nath, born in the village of Kendra," came Yani's sharp reply.

The man paused in his tracks at the door of the throne room. He turned around and cast his gaze on Yani. "So I am the one with the sword and you are the learned, you have proved that. Well done, Rajkumar, it has been a while since someone saw through," said raja Kabala. Yani gave a bow in return, one full of humility.

"Now that we are formally introduced, state your purpose of visit to Nada," said Kabala as he took his place on the golden throne.

"News has reached my ears that a man called Bodhan has approached you recently?" asked Yani.

"I presume that you have bribed someone from my court for this news?"

Yani remained silent and Kabala asked him, "But that is not the point. The question is, do you know who Bodhan is?"

"He is one of the Nimit if that is what you are hinting at," replied Yani.

"You are intelligent for a northerner and within moments you have placed yourself in my good graces , but I respect the privacy of my guests. Especially the ones who hail from orders stronger than kings and kingdoms."

"Stronger than kings and kingdoms?" asked Yani. "Does that even include Nisarga?" he smiled.

"Lord Kubha's daughter was supposed to be married to you but it has been called off and Himadri is but a small kingdom," replied Kabala with a sour smile on his face. Yani was taken aback.

"Surprised? I am a raja and a *dasshu* (pirate). I thrive and survive on information." Yani waited for the king to complete. "Make a better offer if you can, though I doubt that you have any other way to sway me from my stand," he added.

It bemused Yani; the man was scared of consequences, yet he was open to propositions.

"You like to play dice, don't you Raja Kabala?" asked Yani.

"Yes, I do, but what does that has to do with anything?"

"What makes you bet before you roll the dice? What are the odds against your sure win?" asked Yani.

"I don't even roll the dice without knowing the stakes," replied Kabala firmly.

"Then, let me raise the stakes for you," smiled Yani.

"For what I am about to tell you is not even for the ears of Kings, but in such things lie great opportunities – opportunities that can even unite kingdoms broken by old feuds."

Kabala's eyes became wide but he controlled himself. "Go on," he said calmly.

"Yes, I intend to, but before I continue, I will also need something from you," said Yani with an uncanny smile on his face.

"And what is that?"

"Well, when the time comes, I want you to do nothing."

"Nothing? You are willing to share your secret with me in return for *nothing?*" asked Kabala surprised.

"Exactly," replied Yani calmly.

"Well then let me tell you, that if in doing this *nothing,* I see my ship sinking, then it shall be yours which sinks first."

"Then for our ships to not sink at all, our first step lies in finding a man who is here in Nada. Or so I hope. He might have left by now, but as the condition of the western land detoriates and the rumor of war spreads, it is very unlikely for him to have found safe passage. Even if he has left, he won't be too far. You will also find that he is the reason of the Nimit's presence in Nada," said Yani.

"Who is this man?" asked Kabala.

"Agni," replied Yani with a hint of a cruel smile on his face.

The Myriad Ways of Destiny
(The Land of the Rising Sun)

It had been three days since they reached Nada and a solution was yet to fathom itself. They had visited the docks repeatedly, but hadn't found any trader who was willing to venture north — the route to Alexandria lay shut. They had failed to persuade any of the charted captains and they did not have enough mudras to buy a ship, let alone hire hands for it. Sidak had been too cautious of late and had even asked Agni to lend him his sword for inspection.

"This is ridiculous. We have come so far to have only been bogged down by a fucking war," complained Vrish. "Look at those damned ships! They will sail to every god-forsaken corner of Gaya except the place we need them to."

"We only need someone to take us to Scavenger Bay; we can easily make our way north from there," said Sidak.

"We can't wait here forever, there must be someone," said Agni.

"We can go to Ilion and then take the inland routes. The map shows it to be a longer route, but it is possible," said Vrish.

"It has more risk than it's worth. Ilion falls under the jurisdiction of the Abode," replied Sidak.

He sat there shaking his head. "We will have to wait here until something turns up. There is no other choice," sighed Sidak.

Param sat there like a mute spectator. Agni couldn't help but notice that he wasn't the same man that he had met some time back at Himadri.

In the meantime, a servant boy brought in the steaming rice and chicken broth.

"At least something's working in our favour," stated Vrish and rolled up his sleeves.

"What was my father like Guruji?" Agni asked suddenly.

Sidak poured the broth on the rice and replied calmly, "Well, I have met him on a few occasions and they have been brief. He was a strong and patient human being, much like you. You even have his eyes."

Agni gave a slow nod. "Solon had said the same."

"Let go of me," came a feminine voice and it made them turn their heads. Agni saw a young woman surrounded by four men and an old man held by his arms by two others in the corridor outside their room.

"She has some fight in her, I like the ones that wriggle," mocked one of them.

"Let go of me and you will have more than a fight," threatened the old man and the other's guffawed. There was dull thud as one of them landed a punch on his stomach.

Agni was about to stand up when he felt Sidak's hand on his. "Not our fight, Agni. We will see many such things in our long journey. We cannot draw attention."

"You are right," replied Agni. "I will most certainly give it a thought but not today."

Then he started walking. "You coming, Vrish?"

"Right behind you," he said cracking his knuckles. "Save some for me," said Vrish to Sidak and Param as he got up.

Agni and vrish had just reached the group when someone called out, "Up to your old rotten self again Vasu?" All of them stopped laughing. An old man walked out from one of the adjacent liquor shops, clad in exotic silks, heavily bearded with a white turban on his head.

"You stay out of this old man," said the man called Vasu.

"Then why don't you leave the little lady alone and get out of my docks," a clear grin on his face matched the beady eyes heavy with sura.

"The docks are for every sailor's son, you don't have your name on it old man," croaked one of Vasu's aides.

"I do not see your father's name on your face either son," the old man tweaked his nose with an odd grin to his face.

The man took a step forward but was stopped by Vasu's outstretched hand.

"You talk too much for your own good, you do not own this place anymore," warned Vasu.

"I owned it from the very day your father gave ground. Though he was my enemy but this much I can say still that he is better off dead than seeing you running wild."

Vasu grabbed him by his collar. "I can cut off that tongue of yours right now if I want to."

"That wouldn't be wise," Agni's interfered.

Vasu and the others turned towards them. Then a smile spread across Vasu's face as he sized up Agni and Vrish.

"Where did you get these two, Girish? Boys dressed like maids." His aides guffawed. The old man Girish was staring at the boys himself, clueless of their identities.

"Now which one of you two is going to sing for me?" Vasu asked with an insidious smile on his face.

Agni suddenly unsheathed his blade and was on Vasu even before he could draw his, the edge glistening on the apple of his throat.

"You talk too much for a man with the wits of a fool and the reflexes of an amateur. I could carve you in two even before you can open that hole of a mouth."

Vasu was staring at Agni in cold blood, as sweat trickled down his neck on the flat of the blade but not a single word escaped his mouth. There was complete silence.

"Run off now before I change my mind," said Agni in hushed whispers as he lowered his blade.

Vasu took a step back. "That was a very stupid thing you did now, a very stupid thing," he said as he rubbed his neck and walked away followed by his men.

"He is right, you know. No one messes with Vasu except me," smiled the old man. "But one thing I must say, you know how to use that thing you carry."

"You have a very weird way of saying thanks, old man," stated Vrish.

The old man laughed. "You two are not from around here, are you?" he asked and Agni shook his head.

"Well then I must thank you lads, now as that is out of the way, let us introduce ourselves," he declared. My name is Girish, but you can call me 'Veer Dasshu'.

▼

The word of the brawl had spread faster than fire. Agni and the others were invited by Girish to have a drink with him. He seemed a bit different from the two bits sailors but there was something amiss. He had been glancing at Sidak incessantly. Agni saw a bunch of scarred brutes approach them led by a woman.

"Yours?" he asked. The woman walked up straight to Girish without paying any heed to the others.

"Didn't I tell you not to mess with Vasu when you are alone?" she barked.

"You worry too much about your old man. Wish could say the same for your brother but I am not that old yet girl."

"You are also not that young anymore and Vasu grows bolder every day. And these sorry pieces of shit here won't even lift a finger if it comes to that," she thundered.

"But some will, like this bunch over here. They came to my rescue if you put it that way," he chuckled.

She shifted her gaze towards them, a hint of suspicion in her eyes.

"And who might they be? I haven't seen them around," she chewed out those words.

"Don't speak as if they are not here. Meet Agni, Vrish and...I forgot the names of the others," he smiled. "Agni, Vrish, meet my daughter, Nikita."

Param was the one to speak. "My master's name is Maha..."

"Sidak, Guru Sidak," Sidak cut in quickly. Girish's smile was gone for a moment, but it returned soon.

"These four are my fellow companions, including Param here."

"What about you two?" she asked shifting her glance to the girl and old man the party had rescued from Vasu.

"My name is Marut and this is my disciple, Charvi."

"Two Gurus! See, I am in civilized company after all, exactly what you wanted," grinned Girish.

"Hmm... and what are the Gurus doing here, in a place like Nada?" she asked.

"We are heading towards the Land of the Setting Sun," replied Charvi.

Agni and Vrish looked at her, and then at each other.

"Anywhere specific? It's a big place."

"Leu," cut in Marut. "Actualy we are members of Sriti Kendra (Sanctum of Memories). We are heading there to record the events of the war as they unfold, its economic impact and also to find the reasons if possible."

"So you are risking your neck for just that?" she asked with a straight smile on her face.

"It's our duty," replied Marut curtly. The woman did not move her gaze, her lingering smile said it all.

"And what's your story?" she asked looking at Sidak.

"Our destination is also Leu but our purpose is slightly different from that of Guru Marut. We are heading there to dissolve the trade deadlock."

"Trade deadlock?" she asked with a discerning look on her face.

"Yes, we are members of the trade union of Himadri and we are heading to Leu to talk to King Crixus on behalf of King Adhirath," replied Sidak.

"Aren't your sorts supposed to escorted by guards or something?" asked one of Girish's men.

Sidak had a half smile on his face. "If you are trying to enter a mouse hole without drawing the cat's attention, then what do you do? Do you sneak in or start a parade? We are here, I believe, for the same reason as Guru Marut; no ships will sail to Leu from the other ports except Nada."

"Then you came to the wrong place," replied the woman curtly. "You won't find any ships here willing to sail even to Scavenger Bay."

"Except us," added Girish. "But it will cost you a lot."

"Father…"

Girish raised his hand and for the first time Agni saw the seriousness on the man's face.

"How much?" asked Marut.

"A hundred mudras each for passage and the gold upfront."

"Agreed," was Charvi's ecstatic reply. Girish looked at Sidak who gave a nod after a brief pause.

"Excellent. You fellows are lucky; a day late and we would have been gone. We set sail tonight, meet us at the west end by the eighteenth bell and don't forget the gold," smiled Girish.

"We thank you," said Sidak.

"Us too," added Marut.

"No need for that, the gold will do. Farewell for now, we have a journey ahead of us and may Trinetra bode us well," said Girish and walked out of the tent followed by his men. But he cast back one final glance as he left.

Marut gave them a suspicious glance and started walking.

"Thank you for your help back there," said the girl Charvi and ran off to her master even before they could reply.

"I am tired of meeting weird people for today, let us go back," sighed Vrish.

"That man Girish seemed allright," declared Agni.

"No Agni," said Sidak. "The 'Veer Dasshu' is a legend for all the wrong reasons. Don't let his appearance fool you."

Agni saw the darkness in Sidak's eyes and felt concerned himself. But he knew that they had no other choice or else Sidak wouldn't have agreed to it. His father trusted him and so should he.

"Why did you do that, father? They were lying, it was clear as daylight," Nikita questioned Girish and he jumped back to his senses.

"Hush girl, you are yet to learn the art of trading," replied Girish.

"What art of trading? We could have made that gold in four trips and with the war now, in three," she spat back.

Girish stopped. "Three trips! We will be lucky if we can make another one after this. This is the lull before the storm. Wars do not end with one battle and it will be the same for this one too."

Nikita fell silent. Girish started walking. He knew he had tamed the storm in her heart while another raged in his.

'How can it be?' he thought in silence.

▼

In the Land of the Setting Sun

The sky was darkened by the fumes of the dark pits. The small cracks on the ground eventually led to the bigger ones. There were fires burning in the hearth, the light was clear in the thick cover of the night. The enchanted tower of 'Mirror Way' stood looming over the rugged landscape. It was the least populated part of the Land of the Setting Sun for the dark forces spawned there in ways unimaginable to man. Even the servants lived there in fear as the Dark Guardians roamed the land after nightfall, the minions of Lord Dark.

Uncanny to the ways of this dark realm, two children, one boy and another a girl, made their way through the darkness of the night through the small caverns of the jagged rocks, the mountain of Lethe stood behind the peaking tower like titanic spectators and the river of Karia raged angrily somewhere far away.

"We must be getting closer, I can feel my powers lessening, my Lord," said the girl.

The boy walked on with haste. Then suddenly he came to a halt in front of a giant rock. He waved his hand and the rock moved from its place. There was a dark cave which led to narrow passage. They made their way from there.

"I feel scared," said the girl.

"It is just the feeling of our hosts," said the boy as walked in boldly. Moments passed and they found themselves in a small room with a high ceiling. There was a stone throne in front of them and a powerful aura was being emitted from it.

The boy moved in closer but the girl stayed rooted to her spot.

"Is that him?" she asked in a hushed voice. The boy went closer to the throne but the black aura started to swirl. He closed his eyes and then when he opened them, the aura was gone. The boy was glowing in the darkness. And on the throne sat a man, weary and old. His hair grey; his eyes white and lifeless. His jaws hung from the joints and his mouth was open and dry.

"It is devoid of life, it's just a corpse. I do not understand," said the girl.

The boy stood there silent, a wry look on his face and his dreary eyes fixed on the figure in front of him.

"Lord Light?" spoke the girl. But there was no answer.

The Escape and the New Tide
(The Land of the Rising Sun)

The night slowly approached as the last rays of the sun retreated to darkness. The salt breeze picked up and the torches were lit. Unlike the other cities, Nada came alive after nightfall. The streets were full of drunks and brawlers as the children played near the shanties. The women were seen setting up stalls and the scent of fried fish filled the air, the evening catch now ready to eat.

Agni looked out of the window; their sacks lay packed in a corner. The waves crashed on the rocks drowning the noise of the lively city from time to time. It was the fifteenth bell hour and their meal was served. It was to be their last in the Land of the Rising Sun for their return was unsure.

'I will make you see the wonders of this world where beauty lies in the oddest of places.' She had whispered in his ears a long way back in what seemed like an eternity. It still brought a smile on his face.

He could still feel her warmth and the sweetness of her breath. But now life was like an ever changing mirage which astounds the brazen observer while it is only his senses that helps him to hold on to what he feels dear. He could see a dream unfolding in front of his eyes as he looked on for the both of them for she was always in his heart.

"It is beautiful out there, isn't it?" asked Sidak.

Agni nodded. "The world is so different out here, even the sea beats in a different rhythm."

"The world is a beautiful place and if you stare at it for long, it will give you respite," smiled Sidak.

"I only wish to live long enough to see things," slurred Vrish as he downed another cup.

Agni remained silent for he knew that unlike him, his friend had something to return for.

'An unfinished song always yearns for its final note.'

"Agni ji," came a voice. He turned and saw the subtle Banshi standing near the door. He added 'Ji' after their name when he was generously tipped before the departure.

"What is it Banshi?" asked Agni.

"Umm… there are a few men outside and they wanted to speak to ya," he said.

Agni looked at Sidak and their smiles were gone.

"Did they give any names?" asked Sidak alarmed.

"No, but they said that they are delivering a message from some Rajkumar, Yani I believe was the name," he said grinning stupidly.

"And how did they know that we are here Banshi?" asked Vrish banging his fist on the table.

The grin was wiped away as Banshi swallowed.

"They are Rajaji's men…and…and inlanders are not so common here. I didn't tell them, I swear," he stammered.

"You fool," thundered Vrish.

Agni raised his hand, "How many?" he asked calmly.

"Only two."

Agni thought for a moment.

"You go and ask them to hand over the message to you," commanded Agni.

"And what if they don't?" he quipped.

"Then tell them to piss off," chided Vrish.

"Isn't that a bit risky?" whined the poor man.

"You do as you are told, or else I will make sure that nothing is left to risk," blasted Vrish.

Banshi scurried off like a rat.

"This is not right, Agni," said Vrish.

"He has helped us before, Vrish."

The door opened harshly threatening to come loose from its hinges. Two men walked in, one of them holding Banshi by his neck.

"We don't have time for your games and neither do you," he let go and Banshi ran off as fast as his old legs would carry.

"You have found your way in, so what are you waiting for," said Agni calmly.

"The Nimit are coming," spoke the man bluntly. "Rajkumar Yani asks you to leave immediately and wishes to aid you in your escape." He took out Yani's signet ring and showed it to them.

"And how does your Rajkumar know this?" asked Vrish. The man did not even spare him a glance.

"Follow the back alley of this inn, head towards Vindu Marg and then cut through the slums. Make your way towards the cremation ground, you will find the docks from there. The Rajkumar will make sure that the way remains safe."

The men turned around and left without further adieu. Agni stood there silent.

"It's a trap," blurted out Vrish.

"If Yani wanted us to get caught, he could have done that back at Himadri. Even if you are right for one moment, then what does he have to gain from this?" asked Agni.

"I don't know," Vrish almost shouted. "But what did Adhirath gain by letting Solon kill my entire family, your fiancée?" He said pointing at Agni.

"They are not the same, Vrish," replied Agni.

"But this raises too many questions," spoke Sidak at last, opening his eyes.

"How did the Nimit come to know of our plan? If there is nothing in this for the Rajkumar, then why is he taking such a risk?" he asked.

"Because my departure will solve all his problems," said Agni at last. Then he told them everything Yani had said on the night they had left Himadri. How Bodhan was holding him and King Adhirath in a bargain which depended on his capture.

"I see," said Sidak after a brief pause. Vrish looked away without a word.

Agni gave out a deep breath. "Listen all, please. If the Nimit are here and they are as cunning as Guruji says, then this is our best chance. The docks will be heavily guarded then and slipping past without help will not be easy. But this choice is not for me to make alone. I will need you all."

Sidak gave a slow nod. "I believe Agni is right. What better choice do we have?"

Agni walked up to Vrish and placed a hand on his friend's shoulder. "I need you to trust me, my friend. Please."

Vrish sighed. "I still think this is a bad idea."

"Yes, it is, and only friends like you do stupid things for friends," said Agni with a meaningful smile on his face

▼

Bodhan opened the door and came face to face with two of Yani's men.

"Move," he said gruffly.

"Let him in and close the door on your way out," commanded Yani.

The men left and they were alone inside the room.

"Is it done?" he asked.

"Yes, it is," replied Yani without looking at him.

"And are you sure he will fall for it?" he asked again.

"I have known him since we were children; he trusts me."

It brought a thin smile on Bodhan's face. "Yet you betray him so easily?"

Yani fiddled with the pages of a book. "Himadri is more important than one man. I believe you remember our bargain?" asked Yani.

Bodhan sat down. "If your plan succeeds and we catch him, then I promise that Himadri will be left out of the Nimits' plans."

"And we will never see you again," added Yani.

"Ever," replied Bodhan smiling.

Yani gave out a deep breath of remorse. "Very well then, we shall proceed as planned. You will disperse your men all around the city so that we can make them believe that they are not walking into a trap while you shall wait with me and a few of your best on the cremation ground."

Bodhan chortled.

"What is so funny?" asked Yani eyeing the man with reproach.

"A few days back, you did not even know the truth about yourself and now you are deciding upon the fate of others," said Bodhan with a mocking smile. "There is hope for you after all."

Yani did not reply for he knew what needed to be done.

▼

"They are everywhere," said Param as he craned out his neck. Agni and the others stood near the crossing of Vindu Marg, the dark alley looming behind them.

"We should have taken the way through the cascades," said an irritated Vrish. "This road was supposed to be safe."

"No one can predict the movements of the preachers; the Rajkumar is not at fault here Vrish. Besides, we have no time to turn back or else we will miss the ship," replied Sidak.

"They will leave soon," replied Agni calmly.

The clock ticked and still there was nothing. The preachers stood there, idle.

"Guruji?" called an anxious Param staring at his master. Sidak remained silent, yet the worry was clear on his face.

Agni suddenly felt a strange sensation, that feeling of being watched. He quickly shifted his gaze from one point to another and then he froze.

A pair of eyes was staring at him incessantly; but then he quickly recognized her. It was the same girl, Charvi. She stood near one of the stalls with her Guru beside her.

Agni kept his eyes transfixed on hers and then slowly shifted his gaze to one of the preachers. Then he met her gaze again. She looked the way he wanted him to. But then her Guru started walking and she followed. Agni gave a sigh.

Suddenly, there was a shrill scream of a woman which startled him. "Fire, fire," the words reached his ears. He saw many people rush past the alley and soon the armed preachers followed. He peeked and saw Charvi screaming at the top of her voice pointing at a distance and people had started gathering around her as her Guru was staring in that direction as well.

"Come," said Agni and rushed towards the other side of the streets.

"Wait," shouted a bewildered Vrish and ran after him.

"Agni," called out Sidak but he was already in the open. He looked to his right and saw that a huge crowd had gathered at a distance as predicted and the preachers were in it. The word 'fire' had drawn their attention.

"Thank you, Charvi," he whispered to himself as the slums appeared a few steps away from them.

▼

They ventured forth into the cremation ground. The ungodly aura of that place gave Agni the creeps. He looked around; the ever consuming darkness seemed to have intensified there or was it his mind playing tricks on him.

There was that odd gut feeling, 'Something is not right.'

"The boy proved himself smarter than I thought," came a husky voice. They stopped dead in their tracks. The man standing in front of them was broad-shouldered, dressed in white yet the scars were visible on his chest. A man stained by blood and born for war.

Agni looked sideways and saw more shadows moving in the dark.

"Two on our left and three on our right at the least," said Param in a hushed voice.

Agni looked at Vrish and saw that same helplessness which had burnt his heart that night. He felt like slapping himself.

"You must be Bodhan," he said looking at him.

"I see that Yani has mentioned me before, what else did he say?" cribbed the man.

"Did you use Yani's name to lure us here?" asked Agni, though he knew the answer.

Bodhan started laughing, the cackle echoed in the emptiness. "Why don't you ask him yourself?"

Yani appeared from the darkness surrounded by his men and that same rider from that night, Hiranya.

"You son of a ...." Vrish was about to draw but was stopped by Agni. He looked at Yani, tired and wilted from the obnoxious games of loved ones.

"Why?" he asked plainly. "There was no need for you to do this."

Yani was nonchalant. "There was, Agni," he replied calmly. "I had to kill my mewling consciousness for the best. I cannot always live under a shadow."

"Is it better if that leads to betrayal and desertion?" asked Agni.

"You were the one who deserted me. But that doesn't matter now."

"You don't know what you are talking about. He trusted you despite knowing what your father did to him. Do your men know the real truth?" threatened Vrish.

"Hiranya," spoke Yani and the man aimed an arrow at Vrish. "You should learn to stay silent old friend," he said mockingly. Vrish's rage was clear on his face but he went silent.

Then he turned to Agni and said, "Give him the scroll, Agni."

Agni was staring at his friend in disbelief. Then he looked at Sidak who took out the scroll from the folds of his clothes. He took it and threw it at Bodhan.

Bodhan picked up the scroll and looked at it smiling.

"Well done," he said looking at Yani.

"Send out the signal," he replied instead.

Bodhan gave a nod and one of his preachers placed an earthen pot on the ground, barely the size of a fist. He lighted it and a bright green ball shot up in the sky.

"Let us go, Yani," Agni almost pleaded.

"Do not beg that bastard," cursed Vrish.

"I am sorry Agni but this is for the sake of Himadri, I am so sorry," he said and took a step back. "Men," he called out and Hiranya and the others pointed their bows at them.

"Notch arrows, draw," shouted Hiranya.

"We need him alive," roared Bodhan. Agni was in shock.

"Release," the voice echoed like a faint gnaw in a dream. The world stopped.

Bodhan and his three preachers fell on the ground with a dull thud, riddled with arrows.

Agni looked at Yani, his friend had a thin smile on his face.

"Sorry for the act, Agni. I did not have a choice; he knew too much."

Agni started to laugh. "Never do that again," he said as he embraced his friend.

"I am glad that you trusted me, Agni," he said. "Unlike a few."

Vrish remained silent.

"Why did you have to do it like this?" asked Agni but then he saw Hiranya pick up the scroll. It became clear to him. He looked at Yani surprised, who was smiling.

"As I said, I had little choice," he said.

Agni kept staring at his friend. He seemed different, more determined and cruel in some ways.

"Be careful, I can only hope that you know what you are doing. It seems that you have made a hard choice," said Agni slowly.

"I believe that you have what you came for, but how much time do we have before the rest of them come? Or is it not part of the ploy?" asked Sidak. The praise came from his unsmiling face, his subtle gaze was not bracing.

"Not long," replied Yani looking at him.

"We should leave," said Vrish at last.

Agni extended his hand, "So here we finally part our ways."

Yani held him gently. "We never know," was his smiling reply.

The wind picked up as the Rajkumar saw the shadow of his friend meld into the darkness. He felt lighter.

"We better take care of the bodies," said Hiranya. Yani walked up to the spot and knelt down.

"Damned traitor, you think you can get away with this?" cursed Bodhan as he gurgled out blood. "They will skin you alive, bit by bit." His bloodshot eyes were burning with rage.

Yani had a mocking smile on his face.

"What a foolish man you are! Even in the face of eminent death you keep threatening me, is it courage or your fear?"

"I am the greatest warrior of Nimit and I cannot be defeated by the likes of you," he screamed.

Yani had a cruel smile on his face as he took out the same knife. "Life is never fair," he whispered in his ears.

When it was done, Yani stood up slowly. He could feel himself shaking.

"Are you alright, Rajkumar?" asked Hiranya. Yani looked at his hands covered in blood. He felt his innards twist as he collapsed on his knees.

The guards looked away. Yani was vomiting.

The Rise of a Prince
(The Land of the Rising Sun)

"This is unacceptable," shouted one of the three seated on the high chair.

"We lose the scroll and also the boy. Guru Bodhan is dead. How can you let this happen Kubha?" shouted Mahaguru Vajra, one of the three.

Lord Kubha stood in the middle as curious eyes looked on with a hint of amusement in them. The order of the Nimit had gathered once again, the two Mahagurus and the Pradhan, along with the other lesser members. The high society was abuzz with rumors as the Nimit had never before met so openly in clear daylight.

"I tried to help but guru Bodhan never accepted it," protested Kubha weakly.

"And your responsibility ends there?" asked the Pradhan. "Maybe we have placed too much faith on you."

Kubha felt weak in his knees. "I tried my best. I swear in the name of Trinetra. If I had known then I would have never have let this happen. I only tried to pass on the scepter to my successor as I was asked by the Nimit."

"The whole purpose of handing you scepter was secrecy, Kubha. Darshana had said himself, 'The best kept secret is the one whose existence remains in front of all and yet its true nature remains hidden'," said the Pradhan wisely.

"But now everything is undone. What shall be the price, Kubha? Your life? Your family? Or Nisarga itself?"

"Please, I need only one chance," he pleaded. "I can prove my worth again."

The Pradhan looked sideways at the second Guru, Guru Satadru of Nisarga.

"Kubha has served us loyally for many years," said Satadru. "So I believe he deserves a chance." And then he looked at Kubha, "But tell me, how do you propose to solve this problem?"

Kubha's face lit up. "I will seek out that boy's friend, Rajkumar Yani and I will myself pay his father a visit. I am sure I can find a way from there. They must know something more than they have already shared. Guru Bodhan must have believed the same and that is why I believe he went to Himadri," replied Kubha.

"That won't be necessary," came Yani's voice. The murmur stopped and every set of eyes turned towards the source of the voice.

"What is the meaning of this? How dare you set foot inside the holy conclave?" roared one of the lesser Gurus. The preachers started towards him.

"I am Yani, the one Kubha ji just spoke of."

The Pradhan raised his hand and the preachers stopped. "I see, and how did you find us Rajkumar?" asked the Pradhan calmly.

"It was easy, every high born in Nisarga seemed to know of this conclave," he smiled.

"Then you are a very resourceful man Rajkumar, but do state your purpose of coming and defiling the sacrilege of this sanctum," said the Pradhan mockingly.

"This answer is easier. I have something of yours." Yani took out the scroll and many gasped at its sight. The Pradhan's face grew serious.

"And how did you come by this?" he asked frigidly.

"I have my ways."

"Do elaborate. I insist," the seriousness on the Pradhan's face was thwarting.

"Very well then. I shall begin from the start. I was helping Bodhan in his search in return of...," he paused, "...certain privileges. But then the news reached our ears that Agni and his friends were travelling to Nada. We reached there and divided our forces to flush them out and then a small number of ours ran into their group. Bodhan was killed in the skirmish, but in all the chaos, Agni dropped the scroll. I picked it up and ran."

"You picked it up and ran?" asked the Pradhan smiling.

"I am no soldier," smiled back Yani.

"A fine tale indeed. But you forget one thing. Bodhan was the finest warrior of Nimit and the likes of your friend could barely stand their ground in front of him."

"Maybe," replied back Yani sharply. "But there were others with him, also this one man, a guru. He seemed smarter than the rest."

"A guru? Do you know his name?" asked the Pradhan sitting up straight.

"They were calling him by the name Sidak, I believe. Guru Sidak," said Yani. But he did not mention that he knew the name from before for it was his father who had taken him to see the man many times when he was very young. He recognized him the very day when he saw him first beside Agni. But curiosity was still rising in his heart.

"Sidak? The traitor? He was with the boy?" shouted a disgusted Mahaguru Vajra but the Pradhan raised his hand before he could speak anymore. There was a brief pause and the room was set abuzz. Yani looked towards the high chair. Then he saw that the second Mahaguru, the one who hadn't asked anything was simply staring at him with a crack of a smile on his face.

"We will look into the matter and find out the truth if there is more to find," stated the Pradhan eyeing Yani. "But now tell me, Rajkumar, what do you seek in return of the scroll?"

Yani smirked and threw the scroll at one of the preachers who caught it in mid air. The Pradhan was taken aback.

"I do not believe in bargains; rather as I mentioned before, I believe in privileges."

The Pradhan seemed pleased. "Very well, but before we decide on your privileges, let us check whether the seal is intact or not. If it is in its place, then you will be privileged, but if it is not there then....." he paused, "things can get difficult."

The smile disappeared instantly from Yani's face, for he was sure that Agni had opened the scroll. Beads of sweat appeared on his forehead.

"I will check the scroll as seals are my specialty," said the second Mahaguru, Guru Satadru.

Yani was sweating profusely as he saw the scroll being taken to the man. His mind was racing and fear was making its place in his confident heart inch by inch.

"The seal is intact," the man announced.

Yani was stunned, rather in disbelief. He was staring at Satadru blankly but their eyes never met.

"Excellent," said the pleased Pradhan. Then he looked Yani and said, "Ask of your privileges then, Rajkumar."

Yani quickly gathered his wits. But his eyes tended to drift to that man.

"There are two I seek," he said. "Firstly, Himadri was never under the guiding palm of the Nimit and so we have suffered economically. I am the future King of Himadri and so I wish to pledge my allegiance."

"Granted," boomed the Pradhan's voice.

"Secondly, I wish to be given that which was promised to me earlier. Aadrika ji's hand in marriage."

The Pradhan looked at Lord Kubha.

"I believe that Lord Kubha will oblige only out of gratitude for this man has saved him a lot of trouble," said Satadru. Yani looked at him again.

"I will be happy to," replied a relieved Kubha.

The Pradhan stood up followed by the others. "It is settled then, Rajkumar. For your unique service I declare you as the newest member and an ally of the Nimit. In addition to that, you shall be granted a seat in the Senate of Nisarga after your marriage as per the norms of holy matrimony. You shall serve the purpose of the Nimit with devotion and strength. If you fail, then you shall surrender your fate to your brothers. Do you agree?"

Yani stood there smiling. "I do," his words echoed in the marble halls.

▼

"I have heard that Himadri is not even as big as Anu. I saw him from a distance at the tournament, so at least I can say that he is fair looking. But his friend, Agni, he is quite handsome."

The maid Chitrali kept on blabbering but Aadrika was unmindful. Her eyes only gazed at the horizon visible from the high tower of the palace.

There was a soft knock on the door as the maid completed braiding Aadrika's locks.

"Coming," she called out as she opened the door.

"Rajkumar," she greeted with a bow.

"Please ask your mistress whether this is a proper time to visit?" said Yani smiling.

"It's perfectly alright Yani ji, please do come in," floated Aadrika's musical tune to his ears. Chitrali left quickly as Hiranya stood outside.

Yani walked inside, a bit nervous. "Blessed morning," he greeted.

"Blessed morning," she greeted back as her eyes traced the fancy metal work on Yani's robe.

"You look as beautiful as always," Yani complimented and Aadrika smiled out of elegance, yet there was a brief pause. Yani kept on staring at her sheepishly.

"So I was informed that our marriage is to be in three days, before the start of Kalmash," said Aadrika.

Yani coughed a little. "Yes, I was told the same. My father will be arriving soon, but before that, I must ask you something."

"Certainly," she replied smiling.

"Are you content with this arrangement?" There was a clear sign of hesitation in his voice.

Aadrika bit her lower lip and smiled in the process, there was a twitch of mockery in her expression. "Does it matter?"

"To me, it does," replied Yani firmly.

"Then let me ask you a question. Why do you want to marry me? From what my father says, back at the conclave, you could have asked for anything. Then why this?"

"I believe that you have already developed a notion in this matter," said Yani with a helpless smile on his face.

"Some of the high born are saying that you intend to sit on my father's seat," she replied without hesitation.

Yani shifted uncomfortably in his seat. "Then I must be truthful as well. The high born are not completely wrong for every man wishes for power. But there is more to it than this."

"More?" asked Aadrika with a crooked smile on her face, the reproach clear on her face. Yani found himself well acquainted with it, but smiled nonetheless.

"Yes more. Tell me Aadrika ji, what kind of a man do you wish to be married to? I believe that he must be tall, fair looking, brave and strong, a warrior, a hero to be precise and your dream is just, for you are beautiful and the daughter of Lord Kubha himself. But I am none of the above. I am neither a warrior nor a hero. I have always been looked down upon by the poor for being rich, by the powerless for being royal, by the unintelligent for being intelligent and lastly by my father for being a scholar instead of a warrior."

There was complete silence.

"But no one ever asked me what I wanted," continued Yani. "I have always dreamt of a girl whom I knew would never dream of someone like me. A girl who is pure, loyal, beautiful, strong, confident and will love me the most. In short, the perfect being who will complete me. I saw that in you."

Aadrika couldn't help but smile. "Thank you for being truthful Yani ji, and so I must be truthful as well. Firstly, I should warn you that I am neither pure nor perfect, and at least a few rumors are true. I have had many pebbles in my past and I know it can be difficult for you to understand. So I am not the girl you dreamt of."

Yani was stunned by the frankness of her words and kept staring at her foolishly.

"But I never said that I am not an honest person or cannot hold true to my bonds."

Yani gave a slow nod.

"We all have our past, because without it there cannot be a future. So I believe that I must change my dreams a bit," he replied smiling.

Aadrika started laughing. Yani stood up as the smile on his face broadened.

"I am glad that we had this conversation," he said with a short bow and started towards the door.

"Yani ji," called out Aadrika and he stopped.

"The part about the man I have dreamt of being tall, strong and fair looking is correct but you missed the most important thing. That man must also have the will and ability to understand me. If that is there, then I can change my dreams as well," she said smiling.

A wide grin spread across Yani's face. "I will try my best," he replied and took his leave. "Come Hiranya," he commanded and started walking, the grin still visible on his face.

▼

Two days passed by like a storm. Yani stood in the middle of his room while five servants worked on the vest with needles. Hiranya stood there smiling.

"How do I look?" asked Yani when the servants left.

"Nice," replied Hiranya with an uncanny smile on his face.

"What is it?"

Nothing," said Hiranya smiling. "It's just that today you become the unofficial ruler of Nisarga."

Yani looked away smiling as he pinned his broach, and Hiranya said, "Just about a month back I sat beside a confused man on the shores of Himadri. Now this! I never thought you will make it this far that fast."

"'The Raj rakshak', soon you will have that title," said Yani with an ominous smile on his face.

"Will be happy to accept that but I must ask you something?" he said. "Why? I mean I have known you long, maybe not that well but you were always the different sorts, hunting and the other things, you know."

"The vices you mean?" asked Yani.

"Fancy word for it, but yes."

There was a brief pause. "Let me ask you something Hiranya," said Yani at last. "Suppose you are a rich farmer, you grow plenty to feed everyone. You have people whom you can call your own and you are at peace. One fine morning you wake up to see your fields charred to ashes and your people killed or scattered. Then they capture you and release you as their servant. What will you do then?"

"I will find the ones responsible for my fate and wait for the opportunity to make them suffer the same, I will bring fire and ashes to their lives as they brought in mine," replied Hiranya firmly.

"And that is what I am doing," said Yani. "But if I can find peace again in the process, then I shall consider myself more than lucky."

▼

The 'sehenais' came alive, the drums started to beat and the pundits began chanting. The holy fire of the *yagna* burnt brightly.

Yani made his way towards the mandap decorated with red chiffons and hanging lamps. He saw Lord Kubha and his wife standing at the edge of the stairway while King Adhirath stood on the other side. Lord Kubha folded his hands and joined his palm; his face was red and his eyes moist, while Aadrika's mother sobbed incredulously.

"I will take care of her," consoled Yani as he held Lord Kubha's hand firmly.

The father of the bride looked at him with imploring eyes and then both of them blessed him.

Then he turned to face his father.

"You have made me proud, my son," beamed Raja Adhirath.

Yani gave a sigh for it would have mattered to him so much in the past; somehow it didn't matter anymore.

"Thank you father," he said curtly and climbed the stairs.

He looked back one last time. He stood at the top and there were a thousand smiling faces looking at him. There were so many splendors, such grandiose and such subtle taste of authority. Yet one thing remained missing.

'I wish you could have been here, Agni, my friend and my brother. May you be safe wherever you are.'

Then he looked at Aadrika, she lifted her gaze and smiled at him. 'It is time for the past to make way for the present.' He took his rightful place beside her.

In the Land of the Setting Sun

The Lance Tower shone brightly in the pale light of the dawn. Lord Light stood on the highest balcony overlooking the small village of Aine below. The door creaked open as Aqua walked in.

"Do you have any news?" asked Lord Light without looking.

"You were right. The Beast has left for the eastern shores; he swims the ocean as we speak."

Lord Light gave out a deep breath, the desperation clear in it. "We should have taken the wall of Leu and now it all hangs in a balance."

"What will you do?" asked Aqua. He did not answer, his eyes fixed on the rising sun.

"It all falls on his shoulder then. But I must make sure that he is ready before he faces him. Our salvation only lies in that. The time has come to test the strength of our pawns."

The Sting of the Wasp
(The voyage)

The salt breeze ruffled his hair as the timid waves parted to make way for the galley. They were somewhere in the middle of the sea of Diksha and Fortuna. The sky was clear yet there was a high wind. Agni could see the gathering clouds in the western sky.

"Now I know why they never stayed on land for long. The sea, it's so vast and open, it's like a whole new world out here," said Vrish.

"Yet she was willing to give it all away for me," said Agni with a sad smile on his face.

"Then you are a very lucky man. Women when given the freedom of the sea don't easily cast it aside for anything else," came Girish's voice.

He came and stood beside them.

"It is lucky to know love, true love, at least once in one's life. Not all men are lucky," said the Captain as he leaned on the railing.

Agni was staring at the vastness of the ocean. 'Maybe this is what she wanted me to see.'

"The sea is the most enticing ever. Once you set sail, the salt breeze, the high sun and the smell of gold can make you forget even your worst memories," said Girish, his eyes shining like an exuberant child.

Agni couldn't help but smile for he wanted the man's words to be true, but he did not carry memories, he carried along the dead on his shoulders.

"Is this your first time on the sea?" asked Girish. Agni gave a slow nod.

"Ahh, the beauty of it! It is the same as being with your first woman on the first night, unforgettable. The frantic beating of the heart and the eagerness of the eye, but you wouldn't know anything about that? Would you?" asked Girish with a wink.

Agni turned a shade of red and Vrish coughed. Girish started to laugh.

"The boy blushes like a new bride," he shouted and his men laughed as well.

"Father, shouldn't you be at the wheel?" came Nikita's voice.

"My girl is in love."

"Father," she barked again.

"Aye aye, Captain," japed the old Girish.

"But Agni you seem like a fine man, and I meant to ask you something."

"Captain… ship, port side and she ain't flying no standards, not even the white," shouted Kuval, the navigator from the crow's nest.

Girish took out his scope immediately and Agni saw the smile fade away from his face.

"Nikita," he called out lowering his scope. "Put some of the boys on the rows, rip open the jib and the mizzen; let her fly."

"All hands on deck," he shouted again. The mood had changed and all the men started running around like bees. Girish never completed his sentence as he rushed up to the wheel.

"What's wrong?" asked Agni looking at Vrish.

"Whatever it is, it's not good. My father used to say that the Captain calls all hands on deck only when there is an emergency. If a ship doesn't fly a standard, not even white, then it could mean one thing – a hunter or a scavenger. We may have a fight in our hands," replied Vrish with a grim look on his face.

Agni looked to his right but couldn't make out anything. Yet there was that odd feeling.

▼

Charvi sat on her berth, the small cylindrical object in her hand. Her fingers traced the symbol on it, four lines crisscrossing each other with a bisected square in between. It glittered as the rays of the Sun fell on it coming through the port hole. She inspected it minutely for she had seen the same symbol on the pages of Darshana's original anecdote. She drew the symbol on a piece of paper and then she kept it beside her as she took out a chart of old symbols and runes.

"I never thought that someone so young could be interested in mundane things like runes and symbols."

The voice startled her. Sidak stood near the door smiling. "I am sorry, I should have knocked."

"No it's all right, please have a seat," said Charvi while her other hand pushed the cylindrical object away from his sight.

"I have been meaning to speak to you for long now. I saw something like a rune on your journal a few days back at the dining deck, and being a scholar of runes, I was surprised to find someone so young studying them. I hope I am not disturbing you in any way?"

"No, not at all. It is true that I do share the love of runes but I am only a student," replied Charvi humbly.

"That is very modest of you, especially for someone belonging to the order of Sriti Kendra," said Sidak and saw her shift uncomfortably in her seat.

"So tell me Charvi, what kind of runes and symbols interest you?" he asked.

"As I said I know very little of them, so I do not have an opinion yet."

"Well for one, let us take the wind runes and symbols. Do you know the difference between the two?"

Charvi thought for a moment. "In ancient times runes were used as they were said to possess magical powers. But after the third era when it was learned that the cause of the devastation of Gianna was some form of magic, runes were banned by the Abode and so symbols came into use. There were many houses with sigils signifying wind. In the Land of the Rising Sun, the famed house with the sigil of wind was the house of Darshana. It is 'the soaring eagle'. The others are ..."

"Excellent," cut in Sidak. "But let me tell you something more. Darshana changed the sigil of his house in the days of his passing. He had scripted it on his original anecdote which went missing after some time. Now some historians believe that it was the same as the sigil of the last house of Gianna, and it is said that it hides a deeper meaning. The sigil looks like a star with a bisected square in between."

Charvi was staring at him wide eyed.

"But it is yet to be proven, of course," added Sidak smiling.

Charvi was deep in her thoughts.

"What's that buzzing sound?" asked Sidak.

"Oh that, Guruji keeps chakra wasps with him. He says that their toxin mixed with the right herbs has many medicinal values."

"Interesting," replied Sidak as he glanced towards the trunk. "But isn't their toxin fatal if used directly?"

"Charvi, what is he doing in here?" came Marut's voice from near the doorway.

"We were just discussing sigils and runes. You are lucky to have such an intelligent lady as your student," replied Sidak instead.

"Ask your guest to leave," said Marut sternly.

Sidak stood up, "I thank you for your hospitality," he said to her. Charvi folded her hands and joined her palm to show respect as Sidak left without a word. Marut followed him with his eyes until he was gone.

"What did he want?" asked Marut.

"Nothing Guruji, he spoke the truth. We talked of sigils and symbols, we also discussed on Darshana."

"Darshana?" repeated Marut and she gave a nod.

He kept on staring at the empty passage, his brows furrowed. There was something oddly familiar about that man but he just couldn't put a finger on it."

"Stay away from him," he said at last.

▼

There was a splashing sound and the galley turned so sharply that it made Marut loose his balance. Charvi almost fell out of her berth.

"Guruji," she called out frightened.

"Stay here." Marut rushed up the stairs to the front deck.

There was chaos everywhere and the men were busy putting out fires.

"Incoming," shouted someone and Marut looked up. There were three balls of fire heading towards them.

"Look out," shouted Agni and jumped on him. One of the balls crashed where he was standing.

Marut looked around bewildered. "What is going on?" he asked.

"We are under attack," said Agni as he stood up.

"You there," came Nikita's voice. "Help me with this thing." Agni ran towards her and put his back against their only ballista to stop it from rolling around and get it chained to the spot.

Girish was at the wheel. He looked back from time to time and tried to outrun their enemy. He looked to his front and saw the swirling clouds, the maelstrom was not far.

"How far are we from the maelstrom?"

Girish looked back and saw Sidak standing near the stairs with Param.

"A hundred flights to the centre but it will be hard to turn around after fifty."

"Lose everything that you can spare, even the ballista for it is too heavy. In return I promise that you will be able to escape," said Sidak.

"What? The ballista is that which is keeping us alive," spat back Girish.

"Trust me and if I fail you then you can put a knife through my heart before you meet your end."

Girish was staring at the pale and short man. What strength can he possibly summon to rescue them from the seemingly inevitable? But then his eyes became wide – it is *him*.

"This is the only way to save your precious 'Nirgrath' and you don't have much time," said Sidak one last time.

"Nikita," called out Girish but his eyes were fixed on Sidak, he did not even blink.

"What?" she shouted back.

"Ask the men to throw away all the cargo and even the ballista."

"Have you gone mad?" she screamed back.

"Do as I say girl," thundered the old Captain.

Then he turned to Sidak.

"It will take them some time but when the moment arrives, you should be ready."

"I will be," replied Sidak humbly as he walked down the stairs. He made his way towards the back deck followed by Param. He saw them leave, his grip on his wheel had always been firm, but he somehow felt them shaking.

The vessel Nirgranth picked up speed. The balls of fire were falling short and the maelstrom drew closer.

"She is light," called out Nikita. Girish raised his hand and signaled Param.

Agni felt the wind pick up and then the sky turned grey. An impervious vale of mist had appeared out of nowhere and had shrouded Nirgranth. He felt the ship turning but couldn't see anything else. Her sails caught wind but the mist did not move an inch.

"My Lord, the galley has disappeared. The mist has engulfed it and yet none of our navigators saw it coming," bleated the Captain of the warship in front of a hooded figure standing on the prow. A thin smile was visible on the partly veiled face.

"Wind magic, interesting," it said more to itself.

"What should we do now?" asked the Captain of the warship.

"Fly the standard, we sail towards Scavenger Bay."

After a few moments a piece of cloth fluttered in the wind, tied from the mast. The sigil of 'the mermaid' was shining.

"Is everyone alright?" called out Nikita as the ship came out from the mist.

"Where did the mist come from?" asked Marut and saw that the others were staring at something.

He turned around and his eyes became wide. Param was walking towards the stairs holding onto what seemed like Sidak for he was as pale as marble, his eyes blood shot and thin lines of blood trickled down his nose and ears.

"What in the name of Trinetra…" said Vrish but stopped as Param cast his gaze on him, his eyes were colder than ice.

"What happened?" asked Agni.

"Guruji is sick; he needs rest," was his frigid reply.

Agni remained silent and so did the others. Param disappeared with Sidak in the darkness of the stairs.

Girish seemed deep in thoughts.

The dim light could be seen from the far end of the hallway as he ran towards it. A horrible scream reverberated through the inn and it made him pause. Then he kicked the door open; there was no time to wait for the others. The first thing he saw was the blood on the floor. Then he looked up and saw a man, bearded with a mane of hair as black as night. He simple looked at him and then jumped out of the balcony; the wind rose and fell. By the time he followed in his steps outside into the veranda, he saw him standing below on the ground, as if he had wings. It was an open field and there weren't even any trees nearby. He saw his men approaching him as he stood there staring at him. The wind picked up and fell again; there was simply a shrouded mist of dust. But when he had opened his eyes, the man was gone. His men were right there, barely ten paces away from him. Barely…

Girish saw the whole thing from the quarterdeck. His gaze remained transfixed on the spot even after they were gone and the haunting memory lingered in his mind. It was time to make amends.

"Back to your stations," he shouted after a while.

▼

"Where are we Kuval?" asked Girish. It had been three days and three nights.

Kuval had a strange instrument in his hand, a flat stick with curved blades attached to opposite sides at an exact opposite angle, there was also a scope tied to the central beam.

"What is that?" asked Vrish.

"I don't know," replied Agni unmindfully. He was staring at the open ocean but his mind was bent on Sidak. News had come that he has gained consciousness but Param was yet to let them meet him. Agni hoped to talk to him soon for his mind was swirling with questions.

"It's a 'surya yantra'. It's a navigational instrument where you look through the eye hole at the horizon and measure the shadow of the sun on the curved scales. Then you follow the mariners' chart to find your exact location," said the young girl Charvi with a soothing smile on her face.

"Why can't they just use a compass?" stated Vrish.

"Compasses are costly. Not all navigators can afford them."

There was a smile on Agni's face. "You are studying to become a 'shiksha charika', aren't you?" he asked.

Charvi almost blushed. "I still have a long way to go."

"And you will succeed," replied Agni with a smile.

"Maybe by this time next year," added Vrish.

Charvi had a sad smile on her face which didn't escape them. "Well," she said. "I never got the chance to thank you two for what you did back at Nada."

"And you don't have to because you have already returned the favor," replied Agni with a smile. "But why scream 'fire'?"

"See, if I had screamed 'help' it would have drawn a bit of attention, but fire is something which will concern the others as well. So it just came out naturally."

He couldn't help but laugh. "Didn't you face any problems after that?" asked Vrish. She had a gentle smile on her face.

"I have to thank my Guru ji for that, he explained to the people that I get 'fits' like that often, which is not true."

"We know," replied Agni.

"What did you say to your Guru?" asked Vrish.

"Well..." she hesitated. Agni gave a glance at Vrish. "You don't have to answer that," replied Vrish quickly.

"No, its fine," she said. "Well I had to make up a story of drinking sura and hallucinating."

"I truly do not have words to thank you amply," said Agni humbly.

"Didn't you say we are even," she replied smiling.

Agni smiled back in return as he gave an affirming nod. But Agni wondered why she did not even ask once as to why the preachers were chasing them. Maybe all of them had secrets which they didn't want brought up, including her.

"I better go and find my Guruji. He manages to go missing even in a ship," she said.

"Old people tend to do that," said Vrish and Agni gave him a soft nudge.

Charvi laughed. "That's true. But before I go, I wanted to ask you as to how your Guruji is faring?"

"He is recovering," replied Agni.

"That is good to hear. Make sure you feed him plenty of water for my Guruji said that he suffered a lot of blood loss."

"Blood loss?" asked Vrish.

"Yes, the body goes pale and veins blacken if you lose a lot of blood too quickly," said Charvi.

Agni remembered the white face of Sidak and the thin lines of blood trickling down his nose and ears.

"I better go and find him, it is almost time for the meal," she said. "See you two at the table," she said and bid them farewell.

"Sometimes I wish I had a younger sister," smiled Vrish.

But Agni paid him little heed.

'Blood loss', what was its reason? How did the mist appear? And why was Param not letting them see him? The questions were too many.

▼

Param was slowly feeding Sidak from a spoon. His face was gaunt but his eyes bore a hint of sadness.

The door of the cabin opened.

"How is he feeling?" asked Girish.

"Guruji is resting."

"Good, very good. I have no intention of disturbing him, I am only here to talk," replied the Captain.

"He will talk when he sees fit," snapped back Param.

"You better watch that tongue of yours; it might land you in trouble."

"Param," came Sidak's faint voice.

"Yes Guruji," said the man leaning towards his master like a faithful dog.

"Go and have your meal."

Param seemed displeased but he followed his words without another. Girish saw the man walk out and he closed the door behind him.

Sidak lay on the bed silent, his eyes staring at the flipside of the upper bunk.

"What now, Captain?" he asked meekly.

"Who are you?" Girish asked.

Sidak smiled. "I have already told you my name and I can assure you that I have told you the truth."

Girish pulled the chair close to the bed.

"I am an old man, Guru. I have travelled to many shores, both green and grey. I have seen men lust for power, wealth and women. I have seen darkness and have come closer to death than many. I do not have time for your games." Then he paused.

"Despite everything, every god that is worshipped, every man claiming to have seen miracles happen, I have seen none in my long life. But I have witnessed true magic only twice, once three days back and before that almost two-and-a-half decades back, when my brother died."

Then he leaned a little closer, "And I never forget faces, even when time takes its toll on them."

"Is that why you let us on your ship?" asked Sidak looking at him.

Girish leaned back, 'he knew and yet he chose to climb aboard.'

There was a brief moment of silence as the noises of the sea echoed in the empty cabins while the deck was bustling with the faint voices enjoying their meal.

"Do you know why your brother died?" asked Sidak calmly.

Girish eyes narrowed on the sick man.

"Your brother found something," said Sidak. "He found a device from somewhere on the dead shores. But he never knew its worth. It was capable of flight and he wasn't willing to sell it even."

"You killed him for that?" asked Girish with malice.

"What is the best place to hide a sapling?" asked Sidak. "A forest. But if a hapless passerby comes by its acorn accidentally, then it is only a matter of time before some curious mind starts looking for the source. A secret in the wrong hands can turn into a weapon."

Girish rage was uncontainable yet age kept him calm. He slowly drew out his dagger. "And now what Sidak? You are too weak to conjure some tricks and there is no one to save you. Tell me, is a secret good enough to pay with your life? Or is it only others' life that you undervalue?"

"My life as well as the life of thousands is worth keeping this secret," replied Sidak as he looked away.

"Very well, I won't say that I will make it quick."

"Will you grant me one last request as is the right of any dying man?" asked Sidak with a deep rooted sadness in his eyes.

"And did you grant my brother his?"

"Yes. In fact, I will make the same wish that your brother made before he met his end. At this moment it seems the most reasonable. I understand that now."

Girish lowered his blade.

"I want to touch the hand that is going to extinguish my flame."

Girish was eyeing Sidak and then he slowly forwarded his left hand. He was staring deep into the murderer's eyes and saw the fear which he had dreamt of seeing for an eternity. Just when he was lost in thought, he felt a sting on his hand and drew it away. There was a drop of blood on the tip of the middle finger of his left hand.

"What did you do?" shouted Girish as he stood up and drew his blade. But his body froze, he could feel his senses weakening as he saw the pity for him in the murderer's eyes.

"I have an important task to finish, Captain. I cannot let you take my life for my crimes against you. I am sorry," said Sidak.

The whole world started to spin as Girish fell on the floor with a dull thud.

The door of the cabin opened and Param walked in.

"Take this Param," Sidak said extending his hand. There was a chakra wasp on it. "You know what to do." Param nodded.

The Madman from Brahmadesh
(The Land of the Rising Sun)

"Blessed morning Yani ji," greeted one of the servants as Yani passed him followed by Hiranya.

"Blessed morning to you too," smiled Yani as the servant stood there astonished.

"Marriages do change people," stated Hiranya as they started climbing the stairs.

"Sometimes for the worse, sometimes for the good; but one thing it does teach — how to be polite," replied Yani.

"So it seems. But tell me again why are we here so early?"

"Books, my dear friend. One must know the laws of the kingdom if he dreams of being the high senator someday and it is never too early to start," replied Yani as he halted on the steps trying to catch his breath.

"Rajkumar Yani, it is so good to see you here." Yani looked up and saw that same man again. He was standing a few flights up the staircase, Guru Satadru. "I never got the opportunity to congratulate you personally on your wedding."

"Thank you," replied Yani stiffly as he climbed the few remaining steps.

"It is an honor to meet the man who had solved Nimit's greatest crisis single handedly and yet so deftly. But tell me, isn't it too early for a man newly married to the most beautiful woman of Nisarga to be here in the Sikshalay? Don't make Lord Kubha regret his decision," smiled the old Guru.

Yani smiled back with difficulty for what he had heard of the man in front of him was not pleasing at all. Guru Satadru was one of the three most influential men in all of the Land of the Rising Sun. 'Words are like daggers at the edge of his tongue.' The images of that day at the conclave plagued Yani's mind, 'Why did he help him?'

'There was no one who can stop him now, he is not the same man anymore,' he thought.

"I will keep that in mind," was Yani's smiling reply. "But I believe that the early bird always catches the prey," he added.

Guru Satadru started to laugh.

"Well said Rajkumar, but..." he paused. "The question is — what are you hunting!"

Yani's face grew serious. "I do not understand."

"There is a saying here in Nisarga, 'The strongest wall is not that which is made of the hardest brick but it is for the very substance that holds it all together'."

Yani was staring at him; the pleasantries had vanished from his face.

"I will be here in Nisarga for some time. Come visit me at the Library if you get respite from your duties. I will rather enjoy your company."

He looked at the man unsmiling. "You are too kind."

"Indeed," smiled Satadru again.

"Let me not keep you anymore, you have better things to do than listen to an old man's banter," said Satadru. "I bid you farewell," he said and started walking; Yani gave a stiff bow.

"Oh Rajkumar... You may as well want to look into the

'extradition treaty of Nisarga'. I have a feeling that it may interest you," floated his voice as he disappeared round the bend.

There was an odd feeling, the feeling of being twisted that which makes a man feel devoid of wits. Hiranya seemed dazed himself and asked Yani, "What is it with you people and all the riddles? Can't you speak plain?"

"Silence Hiranya," commanded the Prince.

Hiranya fell silent and opened the door for him. Yani walked inside the great hall. There were many there and his ears were filled with noises, but his mind was somewhere else.

'What does that man want from me?'

▼

Yani was immersed deep in the maze of words as his eyes traced each and every letter minutely.

'1.21, Voice of Darhsana, the extradition treaty (came into effect in the year 121 of the fourth era) states that the Kingdoms which are bound by the treaty must handover any individual to the rulers of Nisarga who are deemed guilty in the eyes of her law. Any individual not belonging to direct royal lineage can be extradited without the approval of the below said Kingdoms bound by the treaty. The clause shall accede to those who are guilty of blasphemy, war-mongering and political intrusion.'

Then he turned the page and the names of the kingdoms bound by this treaty came up one by one. Yani saw that all the kingdoms of the Land of the Rising Sun were under its folds except the tribes of Khara, Nada and Durg. Even Himadri was there in the list of the kingdoms bound by it. Yani slowly stroked his hair, the power of the Nimit was threatening. He turned the pages and finally came to the list of people convicted under the obligations of this treaty.

There were many names; some belonging from noble houses while some were philosophers and the list went on. Yani was at a loss.

'Did Satadru want him to see the power of the Nimit? But why? Was he still not being trusted? But then why did the man help him?'

"What are you doing?" asked Aadrika peering over his shoulders.

"Nothing, just going through a few things."

Then he felt the warmth of her breath on his ears as her long fingers traced the hairline on his neck. The book did not escape her notice.

"You do take your responsibilities very seriously. You know what my father used to say?"

"What?" asked Yani with a faint smile on his face.

"He used to say that the person I am going to marry will be my complete opposite, serious and timid by nature. I used to hate him for that."

"Do you hate him now?" he asked smiling.

"We shall see," she replied with a playful smile on her face. Then she came closer to him again.

"Seriously, haven't you read enough today?" she asked.

"Someone is rather an impatient person," he replied with a tweak of a smile.

"Do not overestimate yourself, Rajkumar."

Yani had a grin on his face. "I am a humble man, Rajkumari."

Then his face grew serious. 'Humility', what had it given him? A past full of stares of disdain and insults from the very man he called father. It was his weakness rather than his strength, the same that the likes of Satadru could use against him. How can he rule if he cannot even take the first step? How can he consider himself worthy if he cannot even understand what the man wanted him to see? He must look harder; he must change.

Aadrika noticed the sudden silence.

"What's wrong?"

Yani looked at her. "It's nothing, just a few random thoughts."

"Spit it out," she almost commanded.

Yani hesitated for a moment but women can be very persuasive at times, especially when they feel something is being hidden from them.

"Suppose," he said at last. "Suppose you are good with your wits and you know how to mould words. That is your strength but then you run into someone who is better at it than you are."

"And who is that someone?" she cut in quickly.

"That is irrelevant."

"Then how do you know that he is better than you?" she asked directly.

'Because he has been playing the same game for a longer time than me,' Yani wanted to say.

"All right, you don't have to say if you don't want to. But if I were in your shoes, I would have considered two things. One, do I need him? And two, if so, then until when? I would have tried to learn from him," she said.

"Give in?" asked a surprised Yani.

"What I hold today as a principle need not linger forever; I would have only learnt to see things his way," she winked.

Yani started thinking.

"Come to bed, it is not healthy to go to bed late every day," she said and started walking.

Yani turned around hesitantly. "I love you, you know that right?"

"Don't be silly," floated her voice. "Come to bed soon."

He turned to his books.

'Learn to see things his way. The man is considered to be one of the greatest minds of the land of the Rising Sun. So what is the simplest trick? The obvious is not so obvious.'

'Depends on what you are hunting,' Yani could hear his voice in his mind.

'What was he hunting?' he asked himself.

'Power, but that he had now. The ones responsible, he knew their names. But the truth? Why did it happen? There was no answer. Was Satadru showing him the way? Did he want him to see the truth? But why? What was his purpose? Trails, roads to the darkest corners where no eyes can see, secrets hidden in the mist. Men with changing faces. What leads to such a place? Rather what stops us from getting there?'

'Rules and laws. Curious minds tend to reach out and this treaty was a tool to stop such minds.'

Then it all became clear to him. He turned the pages and started going through the list of people extradited under this treaty. There were many reasons ranging from murdering nobles of Nisarga to slandering the names of well-known gurus. But there was nothing substantial.

Then suddenly his eyes got stuck in a row. There was no name on it instead what it showed was:

An eccentric by nature, captured from Brahmadesh, extradited and condemned to death by hanging on charges of slandering the name of Darshana himself.

Belongings - Mostly burnt by him.

Year of birth - Unknown

Year of Death - Five hundred and seventh year of the fourth era.

Yani went through the list again. That man was the only exception, the one with no name.

'Almost fourteen years back,' Yani thought to himself. 'Was this the very thing that Satadru wanted him to see? But the question remained...Why?'

▼

Guru Satadru was deeply engrossed in his work, the scrolls lying asunder.

"Guruji," came Dobra's timid voice.

"How many times have I told you not to disturb me when I am working?"

"I am sorry Guruji but you have a visitor," replied Dobra helplessly.

"Blessed morning Satadru ji, I hope I am not disturbing."Yani stood near the door with a smile on his face. "I invited myself inside; thought I should greet you first."

A thin crack of a smile appeared on Guru Satadru's face. "Dobra bring us some tea please, we have a guest."

"No thank you but I have already had my tea," replied Yani as he walked inside.

"Leave us Dobra," said Satadru and there was the sound of the closing of the door.

"So Rajkumar, we finally get to know each other."

"The pleasure is all mine," replied Yani quickly.

"Come, sit, please."Yani did as the man said. He sat down on the opposite *ashan* (a small piece of woven cloth used for sitting on the floor).

"Now tell me, did you find anything interesting in those mundane law books?"

"Nothing of note," lied Yani.

"That is sad," said Satadru smiling. Yani wanted to see whether the man was truly as smart as he was said to be. Satadru was staring at him with a meaningful smile on his face, but Yani did not flinch.

"Well let me see," said the old Guru suddenly. "As you delight me with your presence, let me return the favour with a tale."

"Certainly, I have always been fond of stories," mocked Yani.

"Good. It starts with an owl," said Satadru. "It was young, curious and very intelligent. It had a wonderful future ahead with its family. Yet it never satisfied the owl. It had wealth and power as well, but it wanted something more, something which the other owls did not have. Everything around it made it feel curious and the more curious it became, the more desperate it seemed. Then one day it saw a bat flying into a deep and dark cave. The curiosity played its part again. One day the owl ventured deep into the bats' lair. It thought that the bats can see in the darkness and so can he. It went deeper and deeper, to the very depths where the bats hide their secrets. When the owl was there, it saw that there was no light at all. Then it realized one very important thing, 'the bats are blind'. As the day passed, it searched frantically for a way out, but failed. As time passed, 'the owl' slowly faded away."

There was silence.

"The ending is not good. But so is reality sometimes," added Satadru with a smile.

Yani's face grew serious.

"Did the owl have a name?" he asked.

"That is irrelevant," replied Satadru. "But you can find such great stories whenever you want, you just need the right books."

"I am not aware of the names of the ones with such wonderful tales," replied Yani incredulously.

"Then I will make sure that you find a few of your taste. I shall send Dobra with one where you can find the name of the abyss where the owl passed its last moments."

Satadru stood up abruptly.

"Now I believe you have something more engaging to do, the mysteries of odd tales can be astounding. I would have asked you to stay but Dobra is a poor cook," said the old guru curtly.

Yani stood up as well. "It was a pleasure talking to you."

"No Rajkumar, the pleasure was all mine. The mind can only imagine but it needs a set of eyes as well," replied Satadru with a dubious smile on his face.

Yani gave a stiff bow and took his leave.

'The man was smarter than he thought. His words were like a spider's web, a thousand strings attached in different ways but the prey had only one choice. For he was in his game and so there was little choice but to continue playing.'

Bond of Faith or Fade
(The Voyage)

The night screamed of silence as the small lamp glowed in the darkness, its thin flame waivered in the face of mild breeze. Agni found himself sitting on a mat. The man that sat in front of him was dressed in a robe and a cowl. A veil of white satin separated them.

"So here you are," said the man.

"Where am I exactly?" asked Agni.

"That depends upon you; I am in your domain."

"What? Is this a dream?" he asked.

Agni looked around and the place seemed familiar.

"Does it feel like one?" asked the man with a thin smile on his face.

"It's…" he paused.

"So vivid?" the man completed the sentence for him. "But the question is why are you here."

"I don't know, but I believe that depends on who you are?" smiled Agni.

The man gave a smiling nod. "True, but apparently that just brings us to another question," he replied.

"But seriously," said Agni. "Where am I exactly and who are you?"

"That depends upon you; I am in your domain."

"But you have said that already," said Agni astonished.

"Seven times to be precise but this time it seems that you remember," said the man in the cowl.

"Seven times?"

The man gave a slow nod.

Agni thought for a moment. "Why am I here?" he asked suddenly.

The smile was visible on the partly veiled face. "Depends on what you are searching for?"

"My mother," replied Agni abruptly.

"What if she is dead?"

"What if she isn't?" snapped back Agni.

There was a loud noise and Agni looked sideways. There was a closed door to his right. There was that harsh noise again.

"Who is that?" asked Agni looking at the man.

"He is trying to break in."

"Who is trying to break in?" asked Agni.

"That is not relevant. Let us get back to our conversation. If you find your mother," he continued. "What will you do?"

"I will go back to the Land of the Rising Sun with her," replied Agni.

There was that same noise again.

"That won't be easy; he won't let you," said the man.

"Who is this 'he'?" asked Agni, the anger clear in his voice.

"Listen carefully, we don't have much time. There will be a choice like your father wanted you to have. But for that to happen, you need to find your way beyond the veil that separates the truth from the lies. Then only you can find the one, that which is your destiny. The theory of origin is simple."

The loud noise echoed in the room. A sense of dread languished his heart as Agni's gaze drifted towards that direction.

"Who is on the other side?" shouted Agni.

The man smiled. "You may search the darkest secrets in the deepest corners and all you may find is nothing but a mirror."

When he looked up, his face was the same as Agni's. There was a deafening noise and he saw the splinters fly. Agni woke up with a jerk, the Sun dazzling on his face, almost blinding him. The cries of Marut reached his ears, "Let me out, I am innocent," and his relentless banging on the cellar door continued.

▼

Agni woke up dazed and bewildered.

"Don't ever sleep in the Sun lad, if you don't want your head to split open," said Kuval peering over him.

"Yeah," said Agni, all groggy and his throat parched.

'Let me out, please. Please anyone...' Marut's pleading reached his ears again. It has almost been a week since Marut was thrown in the store room and locked away. Nikita had declared him to be the culprit. She said that her father suspected one of the travelers to be a warlock and Marut was the one for there were three reasons. Firstly, it was Marut who was carrying a dangerous species of insects without their knowledge, the one responsible for Girish's condition. The dead wasp was found on his unconscious body. Secondly, he was missing during the meal and the other Guru was sick and bed ridden. Thirdly, it was only for Sidak's disciple Param that Girish was saved from certain death for he was the one who had sucked out the poison risking his own life and had administered something like an antidote. Girish was still unconscious and was yet to recover. Nikita had thrown away the box full of wasps into the sea.

"This one is a screamer," said Kuval. "But we are almost near Scavenger Bay, so my ears won't suffer for long."

"What will Nikita do to him?" asked Agni.

"Frankly, I think she will nail him to wood for the crows. Trying to kill the captain of a ship you're on is a sin of the sea. He will be made an example of."

"But he will be given a trial, right?" asked Agni.

Kuval laughed. "They always are but none has made their mark yet."

Agni's face grew serious. Marut seemed like an uptight man to him at first but why would he do this and leave the trails leading to him. It all seemed like utter nonsense to Agni. But if not Mrut, then who could have done it?

▼

Charvi sat alone on her bunk with only tears as her company. Marut was more than a Guru to her. The man had taken care of her like her guardian after her father left and her mother passed away. He could have never done something like that and the most important part was that there wasn't any motive. She had gone to Nikita for several times in the past few days to vouch for Marut's innocence but she was threatened to be subjugated to the same fate as Marut himself.

The only part she couldn't understand was Marut's absence during the meal that day.

"Can I come in?" came Sidak's voice.

Charvi quickly wiped away her tears. "Yes please."

"How are you doing?" he asked as he sat down beside her.

"I am fine," she croaked.

"I am very sorry for your loss."

"He is not dead yet," she snapped back. "He is a Guru and he will defend himself at the trials."

There was a sad look on Sidak's face.

"What do you know about Scavenger Bay Charvi?" he asked sympathetically. "It is a pirate port like Baluchar in the east."

Charvi looked scared. "There won't be a trial, at least not the way we know of," added Sidak.

Her eyes were wide with fear and then she felt the cold touch of Sidak's hand on hers.

"I hate to say this but I think you should go back."

"I have nowhere to go," she replied, her voice shaking.

"My father left us, my mother and me," her words drew his gaze. "I was still in her womb then. The man that they are going to kill was kind enough to take us in. She died a few years back and now he is all I have."

She couldn't hold back her tears any longer.

Sidak wore a different look than before; there was something different about his eyes.

"He left? Was he a Guru?"

She slowly shook her head. "No, but he was said to be a knowledgeable man. He left nineteen years back for the Land of the Setting Sun and never came back."

"But your Guru said that you two were heading towards Leu to document the war?" said Sidak despite knowing that it was a lie.

"We lied, we needed passage."

"Why Leu? Your father could have gone anywhere in the Land of the Setting Sun?"

"His notes," she replied meekly.

"I see," said Sidak more to himself, he was deeply engrossed in his thoughts.

"If you do not mind can you tell me his name?" asked Sidak suddenly.

"Aranya."

Sidak sat there frozen. He could hear her silent cries of grief.

"Charvi," said Sidak after a brief pause. She looked at him.

"I can make you an offer after hearing your tale. I am going to Leu myself along with my disciples. I can take you there and on my honor as a Guru I promise that I will keep you from harm's way. That's the best I can do."

Charvi sat there dumbstruck.

"I know that at this turn of events, my offer can sound incredibly poor to you, but I believe it is your best choice."

"I cannot leave him behind," she replied astonished.

"What other choice do you have, Charvi?"

"He has taken care of me for nineteen years and in return you are saying that I should abandon him when he needs me the most. How can you even say that?"

"Your Guruji would have wanted the same for you as it is the most rational of choices," stressed Sidak.

"I know what I have to do; it's just that I was afraid and now I realize that I shouldn't be."

"Don't be foolish, they will condemn you to the same fate as him," said Sidak firmly.

She stood up slowly. "Guruji, I appreciate your kindness but I need to be alone now."

Sidak stood up as well. "So you have decided?" he asked.

Charvi nodded and Sidak left the room without another word, closing the door behind him.

"Is everything all right, Guruji?" asked Param as he saw the furrows on his forehead.

"No my dear Param, it is not. When I saw the journal in her hand for the first time with the mark on it, it troubled me but I persuaded myself that she was a curious mind like the many I have met. So I thought of her to be valuable and now she proves to be more than that. It seems that I have made a grave miscalculation being unaware of a few facts. I need to correct that...at any cost."

"Where there is a will, there is always a way – your words which I always follow," said the disciple humbly.

Sidak smiled and gave a slow nod.

The Hollows of the Soul
(The Land of the Rising Sun)

The road uphill was windy as the western horizon darkened. Yani along with Hiranya and five of his household guards travelled to Fort Kup of the southern valley of Mount Gumbaj.

Guru Satadru had sent him the records of the prisoners of Kup through Dobra and Yani found the nameless man in its list.

The ancient fortress of Kup, the worst prison in the Land of the Rising Sun. Its walls ran from edge to edge of the stone chest of the great mountain and inside lay the Narak dwar (the door to hell). It was a huge cave that ran deep and then plummeted into a fall; what lay beneath, no one knew. There was a saying of old, 'Once you step inside Kup, it is not only shackles that bind you and there is no coming back.

"Rajkumar, we better slow down, the road gets steeper from here and the wind is also picking up," said one of his household guards.

'You better slow down. I like the fact that you are ambitious, but Satadru is not the way to go. He is someone to be kept away,' Aadrika's parting words rang in his ears.

The journey was difficult, yet the ordeal seemed over as they had crawled under the shadow of the great peak.

"Now, this is a sight I won't ever forget," said Hiranya as he reared his horse.

159

Yani kept on staring himself. The high walls rose a hundred hands at least, broad as ten horses could have galloped side by side and two sculpted figures of the 'Praharis' stood eternal vigil outside the daunting iron gate. Kup was said to be built by the first travelers from the west under the monarch Rudranksh of the line of Vayu to protect the gold mine from the wandering hordes.

"Riders," called out one of his men and Yani saw the 'praharis' of the Kup approach. They halted in front of them.

"Who amongst you is Rajkumar Yani?"

"Aren't you too bold for just a guard?" asked Hiranya staring at the man.

The 'prahari' cast him a discerning look.

"I am," said Yani. The man measured him from top to toe.

"Follow me," he said and turned his horse around.

Yani signaled his men and they trotted behind the great spear holders of Kup. They rode in silence and soon found themselves in front of the mammoth gate. The prahari called out and hinges clanked, the sound of iron grating iron greeted the visitors to the dreary fort. When they stepped inside, the first thing they saw was the mouth of the cave, the gaping abyss of darkness. Two narrow drains ran from either side, the foul stench poisoning the air. The jutting asphalt rocks and the grey soil truly made it look like the very door to hell.

"Go straight and you will find Daroga ji there," said the prahari and rode off.

"I do not like this place," said Hiranya.

"Me too Hiranya," said Yani and started for the mouth of the cave.

A few moments passed and he saw the welcoming party, shadows in the darkness and the man that stood in front of them was not as big as Yani had expected, but his grey mane and worn out scale armor made him look someone of a different breed.

"You must be the Rajkumar?"

"Rajkumar Yani," he replied as he came down from his horse and the others followed suit.

The man had a mocking smile on his face. "Forgive me for my manners, but we are ill-suited to visitors. We never allow anyone inside except for the ones we really want to have."

Yani gave the man a look.

"Follow me if you must, but your men stay here."

"What? We are the household guards of the Senator of Nisarga. We go wherever the Rajkumar goes," spoke Hiranya out of turn.

The man turned around. "There are no senators inside Kup; there are temporary guests and permanent guests. Which one do you think you want to be?"

"Insolent bas..." But Hiranya stopped as he felt Yani's hand on his shoulder. He looked at him and he simply shook his head.

"This is a bad idea Rajkumar," spoke Hiranya in a hushed voice.

"If I do not come out by nightfall, then you must head back and inform Aadrika," said Yani as he let go of his shoulder.

"Lead the way," he said and followed the man glancing back one last time to see the anxiousness on Hiranya's face.

The man, his host, led him down from the broad mouth to a narrow cave, the torches burning in their hand were the only source of light in there. The screams of the prisoners and their endless ranting echoed through the empty caverns. It became darker and darker with each step they took inside the cursed place. Yani felt the numbness of his hands and the sting of his eyes. They had been walking for quite a while and Yani wanted to ask, but he didn't dare. They came to a part of the cave which was slightly broader than the rest.

"This is where we cremate the dead," spoke the man. Yani swept his eyes only to see charred wood and bones of old. The horrible stench almost made him puke.

"I am not here for sightseeing," replied Yani firmly. The man did not reply.

"Are you deaf?"

There was a pause.

"Very well but the archives are in the farthest corner of this prison," came the reply.

They passed by the pit next, a dark furrow in the earth like an ever consuming demon. They almost had to cling onto the narrow ledge.

"Watch your step. If you fall, who knows what you may find down there. We became curious and threw in a few but they never came back to tell us the tale," snorted the madman.

Yani remained silent, his breath was heavier. They came to another point and there were smaller cells there, the doors sealed shut with one small hole in them. Suddenly there was sound of fists banging on the doors. The noise rose like wave and fell.

"This is where we keep the ones who have lost their mind to the darkness and it is common for it is not only shackles that bind you inside Kup."

"Enough," shouted Yani. "Stop this right now. I am the Rajkumar of Himadri and a Senator of Nisarga. I will not be trifled with."

The man started laughing. "Anyone is no one and no one can be anyone in here, Rajkumar. Kup not only takes a man's titles and name, but his very soul. The strongest arm with the farthest reach can only grasp nothing but a handful of dirt inside Kup. Even bones cannot be found if I don't want them to be."

"I come bearing the names of those you serve," threatened Yani.

The man smiled an uncanny smile in return.

"Guru Satadru wanted you to remember that always. He wishes that your foot may never step on the soil of Kup ever again."

Yani cringed for a moment. Then came fear to his aid; a daunting sense of dread and turmoil wreaked his very soul. The warning was given.

"Now we go to the archives," said the man.

▼

The rain came and the little drops of water swept away the dirt. Nisarga breathed relief after its first spell of monsoon shower. The sky wept as the lamps flickered in the wind and streets did not see a single living soul.

A small candle lighted the room of the upper tier of the library as a figure slouched over the scrolls.

"I hope that your trip was pleasant? You are lucky to have escaped the rain," said Satadru even without lifting his gaze.

"Why did you send me there?" asked Yani, the bitterness clear in his voice.

"You wanted to know where the owl died, didn't you?"

"No more games," shouted Yani.

Satadru looked up this time. "Games? This game was started by you; you rolled the first dice, remember?"

"I don't even know you," said Yani with gritted teeth.

"That you don't," paused Satadru. "But you knew Bodhan."

He stood there stunned.

"Did you honestly believe that no one will ever come to know as to what you did? You will simply walk in here with the scroll and we will hand over Nisarga to you?"

Satadru stood up. "Coincidence and luck are mere words. When they come by, the wisest cannot even determine which factors are at play there and you are very young. So I don't blame you."

"I am Kubha's son-in-law," he mumbled.

"And what makes you think that he is indispensible?" asked the old man.

Yani quickly gathered his wits. "I am the Rajkumar of Himadri and…"

"Are you?" cut in Satadru. Yani eyes became wide; there was abject fear residing somewhere in there.

"I know everything and do not waste your time in asking as to how? You will have your answer very soon," completed Satadru; Yani was frightened.

Satadru went closer to him, his mouth near Yani's ear. "You are an illusion, Yani, a mere image of what is supposed to be true," he whispered. Yani's hand was shaking.

Then he slowly walked away. "Tell me, did you find what you went looking for?"

"Yes," replied Yani meekly. "What did you find?"

"This man had collected all the maps and accounts of the travelers till the third era," spoke Yani like a puppet.

"And did you find any mention of Prasasthi anywhere, the village which is said to be the home of Darshana?" asked Satadru with an innocuous tone. "Did you go through all the accounts of the travelers?"

"It was referred to as the land of the hill tribes in every account," replied Yani with difficulty.

"Good. Now I think that you are smart enough to understand what this implies."

He stood there silent. Satadru was smiling. "Very well. Now as you know this little secret, you are ready. You shall go to Brahmadesh, the place from where it all began."

▼

The night passed by in silence, bearing witness to the secrets of the dark and then a dazzling dawn greeted Nisarga. The rays of the sun danced on the courtyard of the grand palace.

Aadrika yawned and opened her eyes. She was startled as she saw Yani sitting beside her staring on with kind eyes.

"When did you come back?" she asked smiling.

"Last night," he replied with a strained smile on his face.

"Last night?" she questioned and when her vision became clearer, it became evident. His red eyes, clothes stained from travel and gaunt face raised too many questions.

"Is everything alright?" she asked.

"Yes," he replied with some difficulty.

"Did you find what you went looking for?"

Yani gave a slow nod but she kept on staring.

"I will ask the servants to prepare a bath for you," she said and tried to get up but felt his hand on hers.

"Aadrika, I have to leave for Brahmadesh."

"But you just came back," the anxiousness was clear in her voice.

"I know," his voice was shaking. "But before I leave, I want to tell you something. So please stay."

She nestled back in her bed and leaned on the pillow. But her gaze remained affixed on him. She could sense the overwhelming sense of fear and hesitation from his voice. Yani took a deep breath.

"What I am about to tell you may change your thoughts regarding me." She remained silent. He couldn't look into her eyes.

"Very well then. You know that I am the Crown Prince of Himadri and the only son of King Adhirath, but..."

"No," said Aadrika flatly.

"No?" asked Yani, staring at her blankly.

"I don't need to know anything. I only know that I married you out of my own consent; you are the crown Prince of Himadri and the future High Senator of Nisarga. One day our children shall rule the two great cities. That is all I need to know and you need to believe."

He sat there silent and his gaze dropped. Aadrika caressed his cheeks.

"You are going to be the most powerful man of Nisarga one day; you should learn to keep your secrets to yourself."

A thin smile appeared on his face. Then he wound his arms around her and held her as tightly as he could.

"I have many things to say to you as well, but all in a good time. I believe that I did make many mistakes but partly somewhere I have forgiven myself, for it was never my choice. I also had a dream back then, just like you said when we first talked and when did it become a nightmare, I never knew. So whatever it is you want to say to me, say so in a better time."

Yani closed his eyes; the smile stayed on his face.

"Come back home safe," she said and he gave a nod.

"And also, I never liked the color white," she japed.

Yani started to laugh.

The Blinding light of Truth
(The Land of the Setting Sun)

"Land ahead," came Kuval's call from the crow's nest. The sails were pulled up and Nikita was at the wheel. Agni stood on the deck overlooking the prow. The Land of the Setting Sun, right there in front of him, his birth land staring at him blankly as if trying to remember her lost son.

"So here we are, the Land of the Setting Sun. Doesn't look much," said Vrish standing beside him.

"We better pack our things. Where are the others?" he asked.

"Beats me, the last I saw Sidak ji was in his cot."

They walked past the storage room and couldn't hear Marut anymore.

"Trinetra only knows what they are going to do to him," sighed Vrish.

Agni did not reply for it was not Marut's fate that worried him. It was Charvi's. For what little he had learned from her was that she had lost her parents at an early age as well and had nowhere to go. Her fate was almost the same as his; the only difference being that she was a woman and the world was less kind to her sorts.

"You better go and let Charvi know," said Agni.

"Are you insane," protested Vrish. "They are most likely going to hang him as soon as we set foot on land. I am not going to be the dumb pigeon."

"This is wrong. One cannot hang a man based on intuition alone. It could have been an accident for all we know," blurted Agni out of frustration.

"Tell that to her," said Vrish pointing at Nikita behind the wheel.

"Ahh… there you two are!" came Sidak's cheerful voice. He stood there smiling with Param by his side but what surprised Agni was that Charvi was there as well.

"She is coming with us," he declared happily.

Agni and Vrish looked at each other and Sidak filled them in, "We are heading to the same place. So I hope you two won't mind if she joins us?" asked Sidak.

Agni's gaze was fixed on Charvi and yet she never noticed, she seemed disturbed. 'Is she abandoning her Guru? Was he wrong about her?' thought Agni.

"Agni?"

"Not at all," he said after a pause.

"Are you doing alright?" he asked Charvi. She merely nodded.

"She is fine now. Param has gathered our belongings and will bring them up on the deck soon. We leave as soon as we dock," stated Sidak. Agni was staring at him, there was something amiss. First there was his sickness and now he was willing to escort Charvi without any further explanation.

"Guruji, can I have a word with you?"

"Most certainly Agni, but once we reach land. Also, we should let Charvi bid farewell to her guru. There is not much time."

Agni couldn't help but agree.

"Come Charvi, let us not keep your Guruji waiting," said Sidak and led her on.

Agni stood at a distance, his eyes glued on them. He couldn't hear as to what they were speaking of but he barely made out the thin smile on the gaunt face of Marut. Then he saw Sidak take out a small vial from the folds of his cloths and hand it over to him.

They came back within moments.

"So the Land of the Setting Sun at last! We are almost there," smiled Sidak. Agni couldn't make out what was happening; it was so awry.

"Come on, let us get ready to set our foot on land. The faster we do so, the better," declared the old Guru smiling.

▼

The gangway was set and Sidak was the first in line.

"Do not fall behind," he called out as he set foot on land. Agni and the others had to make their way down forcefully ignoring the curses of the disgruntled sailors of Nirgranth'.

"What's that weird smell?" said Vrish. Agni could smell it too, a pungent smell of something corrosive.

Then suddenly there was uproar.

"The prisoner is escaping," someone shouted and there was a sound of a splash.

"In the water," shouted Kuval.

"Hurry," cringed Charvi and almost pushed Agni off the gangway.

"This way," called out Sidak from the shore.

"Do not let the others escape," came Nikita's cry.

"What the hell?" paused Vrish but Param grabbed him by his arm and started running.

Then everything happened in a flash. There was a cracking noise and the splinters flew from the hull. Then it happened over and over again. Soon some of the sailors collapsed as the dock filled with screams and shouts. A stampede broke out. Agni glanced back and saw the same ship that had been chasing them from sea of Diksha. Nirgranth started to sink. He looked to the front as the wave of unknown faces pushed him along.

"Vrish," called out Agni but his voice was drowned in the sea of noises. He was running blind and then he lost his footing.

When he looked up, there was a man standing in front of him, draped in white and his eyes were odd, deep purple and it shone brightly.

"Hello Agni, I have been waiting for you," were his only words.

▼

"You," said Agni, his eyes fixed on the man. He had felt that presence before, but the discerning look and the ghastly tone kept him rooted to the spot.

"So you step on the very soil that took your father's life and it is only fate that the son makes the same mistake," said the man unabashed.

Agni took out his blade in a flash. "What do you know about my father?"

There was a hint of a grey smile underneath the veil. "Does it matter Agni? If it did, then you wouldn't have been here, would you? The question is, 'where is your mother'?"

Agni was thwarted for a moment, his deliberation clear on his face but he could not accede.

"If that is what you seek my dear Agni, then there shall be more blood on your hands and this time you cannot pass it on as an act of mercy," said the man coldly.

"How do you know that?" snarled Agni.

"I know all about you, every bit that you can imagine. Are you ready to do everything that is needed to fulfill your desire?"

'Yes' came a faint whisper which was only for his ears, Agni lifted his sword higher.

"You are more than eager, I see. Very well, let us see then," the man got ready and raised his hand. There was a blinding flash. Agni reeled backwards. Then he felt a surging heat and when he opened his eyes, cascading tides of flames came lashing at him. It hit him hard and he could feel his clothes catching fire.

When he landed a few steps away, the fire went out and there was smoke rising from the burnt edges of his clothes.

"Is that it?" floated the man's words to his ears like a cruel joke.

"Your father was a weak man and the same blood runs in you. He chose to die when he could have survived. How can you be so different?"

"My father was not weak," shouted Agni. "He did what the others could not. He died to protect me."

"And why is that Agni? You were his seventh son, he let his six die. Why not you as well?"

Agni's eyes became wide, "Seventh?" he mumbled.

The man started to laugh. "Solon did not tell you that? Did he?"

Agni kept on staring at him. "I will tell you why. He chose to save you because he was a man filled with the poison of pride. He wanted to become something which a man never could; reality soon dawned on him. Then you were born. You were the special child; the black fire consumed your mother's bed when you were still in her womb. He knew its meaning and so he decided to use you as his weapon. You are his legacy, his pride and through you, he wanted to achieve his one goal."

"What?" asked Agni but he was afraid.

"Making his line the rulers of Gaya by defeating me, the Lord of Light, the greatest of the Seven Guardians of man," he ushered him into reality.

Agni's hands were shaking. The flashes of Solon and that night kept coming back to him.

The man continued, "It's sad, isn't it? A father using his son to mark his name on the realm of man."

"It's a lie, you are lying. He never wanted me to return," screamed Agni.

There was a partly visible and inscrupulous smile on the bearer's face. "If that's true, then why are you here in the first place? Wasn't it the small facts that your father left behind that led you here?"

He stood there stunned for in his heart he knew that it was the truth.

"That blade which you carry is called 'Hearth fire'. It emits the strength of its bearer and also his magical qualities, in your case the dark fire. Now do you see Agni?"

He stood there defeated, his world was spinning.

"You have two choices, one to return back from where you came from and the second to die."

His heart and mind were racing.

'Take the prophecy and run, Agni. Run as far as you can and start anew. Somewhere where no one will know who you are. That is the gift your father wanted you to have, the gift of life and freedom,' he could hear Solon speak from that night.

Then he looked at the sword in his hand.

'This was given to me by your father and as I see it, you will need it more that I do from now on. After all, you are your father's son,' his parting words kept ringing in his ears. '.... You are your father's son.'

He closed his eyes. He was back on the shores of Himadri and somehow he could feel her presence.

'What am I going to do?' he found himself asking. Then he heard her voice, her Malini.

'I don't know but I know this much that you are going to do what is right. I have faith in you for you may not be the best man in Gaya, but you are better than everyone I know.'

"So what have you decided, Agni?"

"No," said Agni. Lord Light stood there bemused.

"There is always a better choice," he said looking at him. "Even if what you are saying about my father leading me here is true, then also I still believe that he wanted me to make the choice for myself. I believe that he wanted me to see the things which he saw. I can understand that."

He paused. "He was certain that I will make the right choice. Do you know why?"

Lord Light remained silent.

"Because I am my father's son," said Agni as he took his stance.

There was a smile on Lord Light's face, "So be it!"

▼

The overwhelming force threw him off balance as the cascades of fire kept lashing at him. Agni could barely dodge the streaming flames, let alone stand.

"Is this who King Arkansas gave his life for?" mocked Lord Light.

Agni looked at him, sweat trickled down his furrowed brows.

"Come at me Agni, show me your strength! You say your father believed that you will make this choice, but did he know how weak and pathetic you would turn out to be?"

"I am not weak," he shouted and rushed towards him only to see the Lord of Light disappear into thin air. Then another wave of fire lashed at him from behind and he fumbled forward. His clothes at the back were burnt and his skin was scorched.

"Does it hurt? The qualities of light are many if one knows how to use them." His figure faded away slowly like a mirage.

"Show yourself, coward!" shouted Agni. Another wave lashed at him from the back and brought him down to his knees.

Lord Light appeared in front of him. "You have come a long way to fulfill what you believe is your destiny. You will unearth the secret that your father has left behind and also…" he paused, "You will find your mother. But tell me Agni, how will you do that? You can barely match me? How will you fight the Seven of us?"

Agni swung his blade half-dazed and it was easily dodged. Lord broke into laughter. "Do you even know whether she is alive or not?"

"She is alive and I will find her," shouted Agni.

"Will you now?" mocked Lord Light and waved his hand. Agni reeled back a few paces. He kept on waving his hand and Agni rolled on the sand like a rag doll.

"You are not even worthy of my attention. So let us make this a bit more interesting."

Agni looked up, his face smeared with dirt, the rage stirring in his heart yet the dark fire was not coming to his aid. Why?

"Let us make a bet. You are trying to find what all sons hold dear to their heart; and for a son with nothing, the mother can be his greatest strength and costliest treasure. So let us bet on the very one whom you shall prize though it is nothing but a vague hope, a diminishing flame of a worn out lamp."

The man took a step towards him. "I will search for her as well and if I find her first," he paused, a horrid look in his eyes. "I will kill her."

"Nooooo...." roared Agni and rushed towards him with the black blade in his hand; it started pulsating. But Lord Light disappeared.

"Remember Agni, whoever finds her first, wins the game," the words echoed around him.

"Show yourself you bastard, come and fight me. Let us end this now," he screeched but there was no reply.

Agni collapsed on his knees. "Come back," he almost pleaded.

The wind picked up and the sun shone brightly again. The world resumed in its normal pace. He sat there, his eyes fixed on the ground, the shifting sands lamenting with an uncanny hum.

▼

The sandy shores of Crab's Nest, a thousand paces from Scavenger's Bay saw the rise of the high tide. A woman draped in blue walked out of the salt water. Lord Light stood up at the sight of her.

"I have been waiting Nereus," he said calmly as he turned around to take his first step.

"Why did you do that Leon?" floated her voice to his ears but he remained silent.

"Do you really intend to find his mother?" she asked again.

"I do," said the Lord of Light at last.

"But why?"

"Because that is the only way. Without darkness there cannot be Light, and without hate, there cannot be power."

"I owe you an apology," said Marut standing in front of Sidak.

They stood on the damp soil of the mangrove forest to the south of Scavenger's Bay.

"I thought I couldn't trust you," said the old Marut as he extended his hand as a gesture of friendship. Sidak looked at it and smiled.

"And it was right of you not to trust me Guru Marut, for it was not my intention to save you," replied Sidak.

Agni sat at a distance, oblivious to their words. Vrish was applying a salve on Agni's burns.

"Are you alright?" he whispered. There was an awkward silence.

"Yes," replied Agni after a pause. The black blade was shining in the sun, his fingers traced the thread work on its hilt. 'I will kill her,' the sinuous voice echoed in his ears. They had found him after the battle was over and Param had carried him to their current spot.

"What use is this if I don't even know how to wield it properly?"

Vrish was staring at the sword as well.

"Can I ask you something, Vrish?" Vrish nodded. "Why did my father leave behind so many clues if he didn't want me to follow?"

"Like you said to me before, he knew that you will make the right choice," replied Vrish.

"And murdering Solon? Did he know that as well?"

"You didn't kill him, Agni," replied Vrish with a hand on his shoulder.

"I did," he said after a pause. Then he looked at Vrish and said, "I had always known what was needed of me to find the truth, but before this, I wasn't ready. Now I am."

Vrish didn't say another word, his smile was gone and there was a worried look on his face.

"Whatever your intent was, you ended up saving me and for that, I can only show my gratitude," came Marut's voice, his head bowed. "And we shall bid you farewell. May fortune smile upon you."

Then he turned around and started walking. "Come Charvi," cracked his voice like a whip but she stood there still.

Marut paused after a few paces. "What's wrong? Come."

She dropped her gaze.

"I am afraid that she cannot come with you for she has chosen our company instead. That was the deal Guru Marut, your life for her companionship," said Sidak.

"What? Charvi?" Marut looked with a hint of shock in his eyes but she avoided his gaze. Then he looked at Sidak's smiling face.

"It was you, you who knocked me unconscious. You scheming son of a ....." roared Marut.

"Do not accuse me of something of something I did not do. I was bed ridden and Param was by my side always," said Sidak. "But an old man seldom loses his balance on a swaying ship. Even if that is the truth." There was an odd smile on Sidak's face which Charvi couldn't see as he spoke in a hushed voice, the words only for Marut's ears.

"Bastard," cursed the old Guru and took a step towards Sidak.

"Please Guruji," came Charvi's pleading voice from the distance at last.

Marut was stunned, he looked on in silence. "Charvi?" he spoke meekly. His dreary eyes fixed on her.

"As you can see that it is her choice as well. I will look after her," said Sidak humbly.

"But why? Why are you doing this?" Marut screamed at Sidak.

"I am doing this for Aranya. I am going to help his daughter to do the very thing that he wanted for her. She knows that you do not believe that and thus you will only get in our way."

Marut was staring at Sidak with inscrutable fear. Then a hint of malice appeared on his face. "You... you are one of them. You set Aranya on that path; you are the white Rishi he spoke of."

"Yes, he used to call me by that name, but he came to us and it was his choice for a truth which he sought. It saddens my heart whenever the reality of his disappearance dawns on my mind, the loss of a dear friend," replied Sdiak with a hint of remorse.

"Friend? You scum," shouted Marut and rushed towards him this time. But he was thrown back by Param. His old bones sent a shiver down his spine as he landed on the sand.

"Please do not make this any more difficult for Charvi than it already is," stated Sidak. Marut looked at her, his eyes wide with fear as his old heart raced. She looked back only once, her eyes swollen and then she looked away.

"Why Charvi?" a barely audible cry escaped from his mouth. A drop of tear trickled down his cheeks as he saw her walk away. His old eyes moistened with the paucity of time.

"This is wrong, Agni," whispered Vrish angrily.

"It is her choice, like the one we made," replied Agni without looking at him and when their gaze met, Vrish was silenced.

There was something different about his friend, something was amiss. His dark blue eyes were not shining; instead, there was a blackish tinge to it. Something was devouring his radiance and a darkness was engulfing him. The Dark Fire was burning.

The Land of Heretics
(The Land of the Rising Sun)

Yani sat beside the large window of the Gyankendra. The city of Brahmadesh bustled outside. He could see the great mountain of Brahma from the distance shrouded in a mist. The green beauty of the eastern shores blanketed with elephant grass unraveled a sense of calm and serenity in his heart.

The people roamed around occupied with their daily chores and the granite roads ran from one corner to another. The small houses were scattered and the large trees on the narrow patches of grass gave relief from the sun to the passerby. There were small tended gardens of multicolored flowering plants and trees grew on the lawns. Even some houses were built around their trunks. The green tendrils crept upon the low walls of the homes of the Brahmadeshis (the citizens of Brahamadesh).

Yani felt that he could spend days just sitting there and staring outside.

"Beautiful, isn't it?"

He turned around and there stood a middle-aged man, clean-shaved and dressed in the simple attire of a white vest and a dhoti. His name was Kalvansh Java, son of Mithilesh and the prime minister cum advisor of the spiritual leader of Brahmadesh, Rishi Ketu.

"We tend to live in harmony with Mother Nature and we love peace. That is why we do not allow any kind of arms or weapons inside the city walls," said the man smiling.

'But nothing escapes our ever watchful eyes for we guard our secrets well,' Yani remembered Satadru's words, the motto of Brahmadesh.

"This is our heaven," added Java.

There was a thin smile on Yani's face. 'Heaven or Hell there is always someone who is ready to usurp it,' he thought and suddenly his heart was blackened.

The large door opened with a soft creak.

"Rishi ji is coming," said Java and moved aside.

A small and stout man walked into the room. His grey mane and hale eyes gave him an aura of reverence, yet there was a strong sense of humility in his presence – a leader who leads not through strength but derives authority from the love and respect of his followers.

"Rishi ji," greeted Java with a bow.

"So this is our young friend from Himadri, Yama," said Rishi Ketu with an unbiased smile on his face.

Yani stood up as well and gave a curt bow.

"We do not follow these traditions here young man, though my old friend here insists that we do, but you stand to be our guest. A simple heartfelt friendly greeting can do wonders," said the old Rishi.

Yani smiled. "My name is Yama and it is good to meet you Ketuji."

"That's better," smiled the old Rishi. "Come, walk with me. I will take it from here my dear Java."

Java was startled, "But guruji?"

"You worry too much and didn't you say to me before that he is here to help us."

Java looked helplessly at Rishi Ketu and then his eyes fell on Yani. It was a meaningful stare, an inescapable one. Yani simply looked away.

"Very well , I will be waiting outside if you need me," he declared and left.

"He never changes but he loves Brahmadesh. Come let us go to the garden, it is always a wonderful place to start a first meeting."

Yani gave a smiling nod and followed him outside.

It was a tranquil place. Leaves, twigs and shrubs grew wildly yet there was order in chaos. The branches wound around each other like lovers and the canopy of the tree played with the light like a little child. A small stream ran in the middle of the garden as the rays of the sun scattered on the glistening cascade. Yani noticed that the walls around the garden were higher than the others in the city and the edifice was entirely more protected than the others. There was also a painting on one of the walls – a fire burning in the hearth while the sages poured *ghee* in it as many stood guard with spears in their hands. The tree they stood under was mammoth in proportion and there was an eye carved on the trunk with many odd scratches on it.

"This painting was made by Dhruv himself. A spitting image of the great yagna performed by our ancestors in front of the holy tree. The Brahmadeshis come here to see it even now. You can call it a symbol of our heritage."

"It's beautiful," complimented Yani. Rishi Ketu smiled in return.

"Come," he said and led him on. He sat on the great roots covered with moss and Yani followed suit.

"It's a beautiful morning, isn't it?"

"Yes it is."

"So Java tells me that you are here to make a trading tie between Brahmadesh and Himadri. You are the richest merchant of your guild and thus this can easily be done by you. Am I correct?" asked Rishi Ketu.

"I cannot say whether I am the richest or not, but I can assure you that I can do it. Raja Adhirath…" he paused, "…is an acquaintance of mine."

"Very good. I am asking this because it is not that I do not trust you, but when it comes to the other kingdoms we have faced many difficulties in the past. Apart from the tribes of Khara, we rarely see any traders."

"That will change," assured Yani but somewhere he felt a deep-rooted disgust for himself.

"From what I have heard, Himadri is also a pious city and you all worship the old one, Trinetra."

"It's true," replied Yani.

"Hmmm. But Yama, before I agree to your proposal, I must ask you one question."

Yani gave a slow nod, wariness as clear as daylight.

"As a trader I think you are already aware that Brahmadesh has no precious resources, but it is not the reason for which our trade suffers. We grow plenty to feed our own and many more yet none will trade with us. The question is do you know why?" asked Rishi Ketu.

"Yes I do. Brahmadesh is called the Land of heretics," was the prince's blatant reply.

There was a soft smile on Rishi Ketu's face.

"I always like a man who speaks straight." Then he stood up and his gaze shifted to the painting on the wall.

"But why? Do you know why we are called heretics?"

"Because Brahamadeshis do not believe in the legacy of Darshana?" replied Yani frigidly.

"No Yama, we believe Darshana never existed and for that we have suffered. We are not allowed to enter any other city of the Land of the Rising Sun."

Yani kept on staring at Rishi Ketu foolishly.

"Don't be so surprised, my young friend. It is common knowledge here. I won't delve deep into it but this is the reason of our suffering. We live shunned from the rest of Gaya like strangers in our own abode. I know it is difficult to understand that we do not believe in the very sage who is a legend in your world."

"But I thought Brahmadesh never allowed outsiders on their own accord?" asked a surprised Yani.

"It is easy to make up a lie when there is a bit of truth in it. Outsiders do not come thinking that we are averse to them and yet on the other hand we know the truth that we are not allowed to leave our land. So in the absence of actual contact with the outside world, this trivia persists in the mind of travellers and merchants of other cities," replied Rishi Ketu with a sad smile on his face.

Yani receded a bit, "I see," he said more to himself.

"I will not burden you anymore with the apathies of an old man, but there is one last question."

Yani looked up.

"Why us, Yama? Why did you choose us?"

There was a dark look on the prince's face followed by an awkward silence.

"Prospect," he said at last.

Ketu gave a nod. "Fair enough, but always stay true to yourself, my young friend, and together we shall prosper. The curse shall be lifted from this land."

Yani remained silent.

▼

"It has been three days," barked Java.

"These things take time," replied Yani glumly as he pinned the broach of Brahmadesh's sigil on his vest, 'one eye of a man'. There was a thin smile on his face.

"What is so amusing?" asked Java with a hint of bitterness.

"I was wondering as to how you shall benefit from all this?" he replied with a mocking smile.

"That is none of your concern."

"True," said Yani. "But then how I do my work is none of yours."

Java walked out within moments as Hiranya walked in.

"He seemed miffed," he said with a smile. "Never liked him even when I first laid my eyes on him."

Yani looked into the mirror and checked his appearance. "Hiranya, the next time you let that scum in, let me know first."

He walked out of the room followed by him.

"So am I coming with you?" asked Hiranya.

"No, not yet."

Then suddenly Yani felt Hiranya's hand on his shoulder. He turned around and saw an uncanny look on his face.

"What is it?" he asked.

There was a hint of hesitation on Hiranya's face. "Are we doing the right thing? This seems like a nice place and pale blood do not run here."

Yani looked at him in the eye. "It won't come to that."

"The wind, the warmth of the sun and the open skies, the marvels of Mother nature never cease to amaze me," said the Rishi more to himself than his companion. "Tell me Yama, what memory does your mind bring to you on such a beautiful day? For it is bound to be pleasant."

Yani's thoughts pondered on the small bits of happiness that he had experienced in his childhood with his friends, Agni and Vrish. Those days were like a closed room in his thoughts and only his friends were his windows, especially Agni. Now he was in a new life with Aadrika by her side.

"I went to a hunt with my friends in the woods of Himadri when we were children. It was a day to remember," replied Yani smiling.

"Life is wonderful when you have companions to share it with and that is the beauty of life," stated Rishi Ketu.

'Yet, in the most beautiful of all places resides the darkest secret, in tranquility lies the path to light and even darkness,' Satadru's words poisoned his thoughts.

"Ketuji, who founded Brahmadesh?" asked Yani suddenly.

"Dhruv," smiled Rishi Ketu. "But he never founded it, he discovered it."

"I fail to understand the difference," replied yani.

"The other cities like Anu, Nada and even Himadri saw its first settlers for various reasons ranging from trade, natural resources and so on. But Brahmadesh is different. Did you notice the banyan tree under which we sat during our first meeting?" Yani nodded at his memory of the huge tree. "It is said that Brahmadesh began from there. The hermits of Aadhar settled right under that tree more than six centuries back and it has grown ever since. Brahmadesh saw many travelers back then and thousands found peace here. But it was Dhruv who led us towards the light after he met 'the first traveller'," said Rishi Ketu.

"The first traveler?" asked Yani.

"It is said that he was a sage and had no name. He helped Dhruv create the philosophy of ultimate consciousness, the very essence of creation."

"You mean God," stated Yani.

"That is one way of saying it. 'One always finds his own way through the forest,' so says his commandments."

"Commandments?"

Ketu paused in his tracks, a strained smile spread across his face.

"A list of religious concepts with philosophical underlining," he stated uncomfortably.

"Can anyone read it?" asked Yani.

"Yes, if one possesses the knowledge of Chhanda," replied Rishi Ketu with a helpless look on his face.

"Can I see it?" asked the prince bluntly.

Ketu lowered his eyes; his deep reverence had turned into remorse. The pleading eyes told a different tale altogether.

"I apologize for my glibness, I shouldn't have asked," said Yani quickly. The smile returned on the old guru's face.

"I am sorry Yama. It is not that I don't trust you, but it is considered sacred to us. It is our source of knowledge and purpose, the very origin of the concept of Brahmadesh. So it is kept under our ever watchful eye within reach of many, but far from some."

Yani kept on staring at him. 'Within reach of many, but far from some, ever watchful eye and the point of origin.'

"Is there something wrong?" asked Rishi Ketu.

"No, not at all, let us continue our little tour," smiled Yani.

Rishi Ketu nodded but his gaze lingered on him for a moment.

The hours of the sun passed by. The door of Yani's chamber opened harshly as Hiranya was trying to pour himself some wine from Yani's cask. He was startled by the loud noise.

"Is everything alright?" he asked putting the cask away.

"Go and fetch Java immediately. I think I know where the book is and I will need his help."

▼

The shadows of the night danced in the little garden as the rippling cascades of water made a monotonous noise. The trees looked on as mute spectators as the night stood still and silent.

"Is it here?" hissed the hushed voice like a sharp wind. There was a lull.

"I think so," came Yani's feverish reply.

"It is said that the secret of Dhruv is kept under the gaze of the ever watchful eyes which means ancestor in Chhanda. This painting refers to the sages of old, the true founders of Brahmadesh and yet it is here, a place where it isn't supposed to be, unworshipped, unguarded and in the most common of places, or is it?"

Java remained silent.

"So what do we do now? We can break the wall," said Hiranya.

Yani kept on staring at Java who seemed to avoid his gaze for some reason.

"What is that old saying in Brahmadesh, Java?" asked Yani.

"Nothing escapes our ever watchful eye for we guard our secrets well," croaked Java.

"Why eye? Why not eyes? Because the symbol of Brahmadesh is the single eye, the eye of the ancestors," replied Yani to his own question. Yet his eyes remained fixed on the man in front of him; there was something wrong.

Then he took his sword out and started walking towards the great banyan tree with the eye drawn on its bark. There were several scratches on it and one of them ran deeper than the others. He placed the blade on it and pierced the eye. To his surprise the blade went in smoothly. His hunch was correct.

"The secret cannot be revealed under the watch of the ancestors so when the eye closes we shall learn the secret. So to make that happen, we just needed to stab the eye," said Yani. "Just like a riddle."

There was cracking noise and the painting on the wall flipped to the other side revealing a secret chamber inside. There lay a worn out book strapped to the inner wall of the chamber. He took it out gently.

"Traitors and thieves," came a loud voice.

Yani turned around and saw Rishi Ketu standing at the door, his bloodshot eyes filled with malice.

▼

"How dare you open the vault? And Java how you could you?" shouted Ketu.

"Shall I tie him up?" Hiranya asked looking at Yani.

"No, we are here only for the book," replied Yani. "Ketuji, you better stay out of this. We do not mean you any harm."

"Stay out of this? And watch you walk away with the book. I trusted you Yama, and this is how you repay me. I cannot do that. Dinesh! Rajesh!" called out Ketu.

Java was smiling, "No one is coming, Rishi ji."

Ketu stood there astounded. "You have shed blood, Java. After all our teachings, you have shed blood."

Java walked up to him and caught him by his throat. Yani was about to take a step towards them when he saw Java's men standing in his way.

"Yes, I have and I shall do so again if needed," screamed Java on his face. "What did your teaching give us Rishi? We are prisoners in our own land. I believed in you like the others, I thought that you could deliver us from this...this rat hole. But you have failed us all."

He let go of him and Ketu collapsed on his knees.

"Java, my dear Java," said Ketu with pleading eyes. "I understand your pain but don't you see the truth. The secret must be kept safe. In the wrong hands, all shall come to ruin. I have seen it myself. So it must be kept safe under our ever watchful eye. If we do not do so, Dhruv shall be lost in the miseries of time and he will be replaced by something created by selfish and sick minds, the Darshana."

There was an insidious smile on Java's face. "Who are you trying to fool, Ketu? I saw what you did. I was there that day but you never noticed. But I won't let you continue on this path. I will not sit back and wait until the truth got out. I will not wait for Brahmadeshis to be enslaved. You gave away our only weapon against the armies of the other kingdoms. You gave away the book."

Ketu was stunned to silence, but his eyes pleaded with remorse. But there was helplessness in them as well. "I am sorry, my dear Java, but that was the only choice, there was a reason that even Dhruv never wanted the unworthy to read it. It must not fall in the hands of the Nimit, never it shall on my watch," he said after a pause.

"What?" said Yani and quickly turned the pages of the book in his hand. It was blank. "Where is the book?" he shouted.

"Gone, and the secret is safe. Only the worthy chosen by fate shall know the truth," ranted the old Rishi.

"You knew about this and yet you did not tell us. Why?" chided Yani.

There was a faint smile on Java's face.

"You won't be smiling when I am done with you," Hiranya took the blade from Yani's hand.

"Is that wise Yani? Do you want to close your only way of escape after murdering Rishi Ketu?" asked Java.

"We will do no such thing," replied Yani threateningly.

"You don't need to. You were only needed here." Java took out his knife in a flash and Rishi Ketu collapsed on the ground. Yani was stunned to silence. He saw the sage's blood trickling down into the stream of the garden and within moments it ran red.

"That man raised you," said Yani icily.

"Yes and it is only irony that I was the one to decide his fate," replied java with disdain. "You have an hour to leave and after that the hue and cry shall be raised. After all, we need time to prepare for the lament."

"You rotten leech," shouted Hiranya.

'I have not seen the monsters or demons of old,
But it is the darkness in man's heart and the treachery of their souls.'

"Hiranya, come," said Yani coldly and started walking towards the door. There was nothing he could do anymore. Somewhere deep inside he wished he hadn't taken the scroll for himself. If only he could have left it there or even let Agni have it. He could feel the stains of blood on his hand for it was he who brought this upon a peaceful land. Now he was a puppet and was not even allowed to hate someone like Java.

"Oh Yani," called out Java. "I forgot to thank you for I owe the high seat of Brahmadesh to you. So in return, I shall tell you a secret." Yani did not pause and kept on walking.

"It was not only me who knew the truth," said Java with a mocking smile on his face. "And you know what the intriguing part is? He wanted this message delivered after it was done."

Yani turned around sharply, his heart was thumping. The words which he heard couldn't be true. Or could it?

The Miasma of Lies
(The Land of the Rising Sun)

The sky was overcast and the season of monsoon had just started, the occasional showers and small puddles on the road signaled the very onset of the season. The bustling city of Nisarga had gone quiet. Only a few vagabonds and drunks braved the high wind, the leaves rustled and the sky changed its colors with the drifting clouds as they seemed endless.

Guru Satadru stood on the veranda of the great library overlooking the city, his old eyes had a faint glimmer, 'the change was about to happen'.

"It seems that this time you weren't able to escape the rain," he said turning around.

"You knew the truth," croaked Yani's voice.

Guru Satadru couldn't help but smile. "Which one?" he asked simply.

"You know what I am talking about."

There was a pause, a sudden halt in the flow of time.

"Why?" asked Yani at last. "Why did you do this to me? Answer me?"

"You know very well, Rajkumar."

Yani rushed to him and caught him by his vest. "I will kill you."

He simply removed his hand as if nothing was said. "And what will that achieve? You will be branded a murderer in Nisarga as well. You will lose everything, even Aadrika."

Yani slumped on the ground. "Why me? Brahmadesh is just a small kingdom. If you didn't want the book, then why?"

"Every drop makes an ocean Yani, do not hold this against yourself. It is true that you had nothing to do with Rishi Ketu's death and it is also true that he was a true sage, but even sages lose their purpose in this cruel world. You were simply needed there Yani, your presence was all that was needed. I think Java has already declared you a murderer by now and thus the Brahmadeshis will rally to Java's call. He will become the new ruler of Brahmadesh and show his adversity to outsiders, thus protecting the secret of Darshana. On the other hand, his true loyalties will lie with the Nimit. In this way, Brahmadesh shall always remain under our folds serving the very purpose of the Nimit," replied the old man calmly.

Tears knew no bounds; he couldn't hold them back any longer. "You own lives," Yani said. "What more do you want? What more does the Nimit want?"

Satadru knelt down in front of him looking in his eyes. "Do you want to know why?" he asked.

Yani looked up; every nerve of his eyes were jutting out like a web of red. Somewhere deep in the black pit, there was a flame.

"This road is difficult. Your burden can end if you follow my commands. But in this path, the pillars of your so-called reality shall come crashing down. A myth shall become more than truth and you will be ushered into the darkness, where your flame is the only thing that can guide you. 'I OFFER YOU THE UNDENIABLE TRUTH IN RETURN OF YOUR VERY EXISTENCE.'"

Yani felt his hands shaking, the images of the closed doors of his childhood came flashing to his mind. 'Underneath the rock lay a cave and in it lay the treasure, but what one needed to do was to reach the mouth. That is not the only truth; the only truth is curiosity and knowledge and that is how only one could travel the dark roads of the cave itself. Because reaching the mouth was nothing but the first step. His heart was crying but he found himself saying 'yes'.'

Satadru stood up smiling. "Very well, then I shall tell you what I told Aranya. Stand up, Yani."

He stood up like an estranged sapling in the crummy soil, a shivering wind and flawed principles mocking his existence. Satadru seated himself in the darkness; the wind was howling as it played its little games with the flame of the lamp, the game of light and darkness.

"It all started several centuries back in the beginning of the third era, with the founding of 'The Abode of the Seven'. It was built with one objective, one alone and that was to bring each and every kingdom of Gaya under its folds, the seven empires of Gaya. The strength of the Abode was indomitable. The days passed by and one by one, the kingdoms of the man fell. Very soon, the Land of the Setting Sun was under their shadow. Then came the turn of the Land of the Rising Sun and soon they were made to bend their knees.

"Then almost after a thousand years of their rule, shadows began to stir in the darkness in the Land of the Rising Sun, for by then the Abode had nestled in the land of the West laxing their control. Rajas, Gurus, warriors and minds from different walks of life united under one banner to challenge the Abode and its armies, and thus the Nimit was formed.

"But the problem remained, the Council of the Seven of the Abode, the seven individuals of great might and their greatest,

Lord Light. The cowls were said to have been passed through generations but their knowledge and strength was unfathomable for the common mind. Even the dying forms of magic of the gurus of the east and the mages of the west were of no match for their paranormal powers.

"And then came one man," he said after a pause. "Dhruv fom Brahmadesh, the seeker of knowledge. He said that an ancient voice of old had spoken to him and he could uncover the secret of the Council of the Seven's might if helped in his quest. He could travel to the Wastelands beyond the Wall of Leu where the voice had asked him to go, but he could not do so without the help of the Nimit. And with that knowledge he will help the Nimit to destroy the Council of the Seven of the Abode."

Satadru saw the fear in Yani's eyes. "It wasn't Darshana Yani; truth is stranger than fiction," he said with a mocking smile.

"Dhruv was his true name and the only one to have journeyed beyond the wall. It is said that he roamed the wastelands for years and then one day he found something there. But before he could return, the Seven came to know of his presence beyond the wall. But Dhruv escaped. He came back to the Land of the Rising Sun, demented and broken. He brought back the secret with himself, but for some reason, he locked it away, never to be seen again. 'Only the one chosen by fate can know the secrets of the Dark,' those were his words."

"Why? Why did he lock away the very secret for which he had travelled so far?" mumbled Yani.

"Why? Why indeed," said Satadru smiling. "The Council of Seven is the strongest force in Gaya, but if there is a power which can destroy them, then it must be more fearsome than anything in this very world. Such a power in the wrong hands could destroy everything, could turn a simple mortal into God. So it needed to be kept safe, away from the hands of the unworthy. He locked it away but never threw away the keys."

Yani looked confused, and Satadru continued, "The keys were his two books, the ones he wrote before his death. It is said that together the two books hold a key which can unlock 'the secrets of the Dark', the theory of Origin. The secret was locked in an encasement made of a strange metal which cannot be undone by magic or any known force to man, but can only be opened by the one who can find the key from the two books. Dhruv had found it from beyond the great wall. He handed over one book to his descendants and another to his disciples. It was said that the worthy can only open the vault of secrets, the black cylindrical encasement hiding the ultimate truth, the black tome of knowledge. The Nimit saw this as treachery and killed Dhruv's disciples recovering the second book and the black tome. The second book was later named as the book of Darshana, the false sage, the name veiling the truth. But they couldn't find the first for it was hidden away by the descendants of Dhruv. Years of torture and slavery couldn't break them. Rishi Ketu was from the line of his descendants. "

'It belongs to the worthy, the one,' Ketu's final words rang in Yani's ears.

"But the Abode being unaware of the treachery of Dhruv came forth and made a pact with the Nimit. The Abode thought that Dhruv had given the Nimit the secret of their undoing, the very thing that was kept hidden beyond the wall of Leu. Thus the Nimit took the opportunity to get their freedom with a lie and according to the pact, the secret was sealed away for the generations to come. In return, the Abode was never to set foot on the Land of the Rising Sun. So the secret was hidden in the catacombs where the tomb of Dhruv was built under the false identity of Darshana. It was locked away and the key was broken into two with one part handed to the Seven. Then a certain spell was put on it which shall let the Seven know if the key was joined ever again. The city of Nisarga was built over the tomb to protect the secret and a history of lies was written thusforth."

"The prophecies?" asked Yani, his heart was racing.

"They are also lies, young prince. The Nimit were asked to write them in the name of Darshana, the false doomsayer, the reason of which was never known. In return of these lies, the Land of the Rising Sun was left alone by the Seven and it prospered under the ever watchful eyes of the Nimit. Until he came along."

"Who?" asked Yani, his eyes fixed on the ever consuming blackness.

"The one who opened our eyes, the true descendant of Dhruv, the teacher, the one Guru. He showed us that the Land of the Rising Sun was never free. The freedom which we marked as our victory is based on a lie, the lie that we a few of the Nimit are aware of, that we never had and still do not have the knowledge to defeat the Abode. A lie which if comes out in the open shall leave everything undone. We made a mistake. We exchanged knowledge for ignorance. What was to be our greatest weapon has become our shackles; we have willingly given up the chance to pursue the knowledge of their destruction and instead have handed down a part of the key which holds it. We have willingly become their slaves, the purpose of the Nimit sacrificed by this illusionary independence. The truth is, they still continue to spill blood in our names, in the name of Darshana and we are nothing less than slaves at their commands, for they knew that with the part of the key in their hand, the tomb of Darshana could never be opened and the secrets of the dark will never come out in the light. We have become 'the moth' that ran into the flame and got burnt. We are still in shackles but the funny thing is that only a handful of us know this scary truth."

Yani was sweating, yet a shiver ran down his spine.

"What does Agni has to with all this?" he asked.

Satadru had a playful smile on his face as he came into the light of the lamp. "Didn't you hear what I said about the prophecies?" asked Satadru.

Yani kept on staring and then his eyes became wide. "He is a Prince?" asked Yani astounded.

"Son of King Arkansas of Athena, the only living Prince of the Land of the Setting Sun," said Satadru.

The cruel jape of destiny was shattering; the truth was indeed stranger than the lies. He who was the prince was nothing, and he who was nothing was the heir of a king.

"Did he know?" asked Yani.

"Yes, after your little trip to Nisarga."

"Why?" he asked suddenly. "If the prophecies are false, then why is he being hunted?"

"Now that is an interesting question, isn't it?" replied Satadru. "The Abode in return of our freedom only wanted one price. The price was to bear the name of Darshana and his false prophecies."

Yani closed his eyes, the miasma was getting thicker.

"The best place to hide a sapling is in the forest and what happens when the forest catches fire. You cut the other trees to find the sapling," Satadru took in a deep breath.

"He, the teacher, believes that the secret of the council of the seven's destruction has something to do with the strange power of your friend. The seven fears it and so they made others do the same. A half truth is more dangerous than a lie. And what one may fear, if he can make others be afraid of the same thing, then it becomes the common enemy. He believes that 'the destroyer', the wielder of the black flame, in the prophecies, handed down by the Abode to the Nimit, is more than what has been potrayed."

Yani started to laugh, his shrill voice echoed in the hysteria.

"What do you find so amusing?"

"It's all a game, isn't it? The one with the better dice wins," he said wiping his mouth with the back of his sleeve.

"A game?" asked Satadru. "If it is a game, then what do you think is at stake, Rajkumar?"

"The lives of your pawns. The puppeteers stay in the dark while the puppets dance. I am one of them like Agni is, like that man Aranya was and someone will take my place later on," he said and spat on the floor.

"You underestimate yourself, Yani. You did what Aranya failed to do. You removed the first obstacle in the path of the unification of the Nimit by killing Bodhan," replied Satadru.

"And did your 'one', the teacher, plan this as well?" he screamed.

"No, he did not. But he wanted Bodhan to reach Himadri. That is why he told me your secret and asked me to share it with Bodhan, so that he would chase after it. Bodhan's failure would have been a serious blow to the Nimit's overseers. Then he would have been taken care of after he would have travelled to the western lands in his fruitless quest. But you did it for us, ended it without much effort and in turn proved one thing," replied Satadru.

"How did he, your teacher, know the truth of my inheritance?" asked Yani as he took a step towards Satadru.

"He knows many things. But he never thought you will prove to be more useful than others and that your hunger for power will push you so far. The human mind is truly intriguing, that a simple man will kill for something what others do not have if pushed in the right direction."

"I am not a murderer. Bodhan threatened my very existence," said Yani but he heard his voice shaking.

Satadru took one step towards him. "If that is so, then why did you come to Nisarga with the scroll?"

He was staring at the man; it was as if he was stripped and his soul lay bare in front of his eyes.

"You see Yani, you failed to understand the very thing that Aranya also did. 'There is always a price for the wrong choice.' And so he did what I thought he never would."

"He sided with King Arkansas and hid the secret. It was he who stole everything from us. Aranya, 'the Sage' as named by the westerners. They, king Arkansas and the traitor, tricked us into believing that the secret was being uncovered for us when the actual fact is that they were trying to uncover it for themselves. They wanted your generation to have a choice. All seemed lost when King Arkansas died and Solon was captured with the key. Even Aranya fled. But fate was on our side when Solon came back with the key and the tomb was unlocked. Then we learnt as to how far they went to betray us for they had already taken out the black tome, leaving clues to it which only Solon could understand. But the one, the teacher, is relentless. With the death of Solon, 'the stranger' as you know him, the way became simpler rather than the other way around. Who would have thought that the son of the very man who betrayed us would step up to finish the job. Our dear Agni helped us in finding the way and now he walks the very path that his father did once. He has set foot on the Land of the Setting Sun as we speak. It is only a matter of time before Gaya descends into its final war of freedom. The Nimit will make sure of that after it has been cleansed, which also will happen soon."

Yani cringed in fear, his throat was dry and his mind astray.

"How do you know this? How do you know that he has already set foot on the Land of the Setting Sun?"

Satadru took one step at a time. Yani could feel his breath, the musty stench of age and a darkened heart. He put his mouth near his ear.

"He who showed us the way, the one caste out of his land by his brother Ketu, caste out from the Nimit for believing in the truth and the true descendant of Dhruv, was always there, near you two. He was there when you two were brought to the Land of the Rising Sun. And now, he walks with him. The true master of Nimit, the teacher of the believers, the great Sage, Maharishi Sidak."

▼

The hushed sound of the steps on the floor remained unheard. The uncharted noises of the night never seemed to have a source, the little pillow talks of the entwined lovers, the coughs and groans of the old man, the barking of the stray dogs and the soft snores of the heavy sleeper. They were all known, yet the darkness had a way of twisting them. There was always the fear of the unknown.

Yani dragged his feet up the stairs of the palace of Nisarga, dots of blood tainted the white marble. His gaze unfocussed, his ears deaf to the noises of the night and the voices inside his head cracked like a whip. The visions ran over and over again.

"The price has to be paid, the price of knowledge, the oath marked by blood," he could still hear Satadru's voice.

"You want him to chop off his right thumb for hearing some useless shit. You want to turn him into a fucking cripple." Hiranya had shouted.

"He who shows us the way demands the ways of old. His soul has been pledged and there is no other way out. It is either death or beyond."

"You piece of shit," Hiranya had drawn out his blade. Then his eyes had fallen on Yani who was holding knife on his thumb, it had made half way into his flesh and it was his scream that had drawn Hiranya inside the room.

"No Yani, this is foolishness. There is nothing worth such a price."

When he hadn't answered, Hiranya had stood there staring.

"You should have listened to her. Aadrika ji was right, this was never the way. I cannot follow you on this road," were his parting words as he had barged out of the room.

Then there was pain, anguish, fear and color of red on white. The screams were relentless as the old wraith had pushed the blade deeper to finish the job. Yani was slipping and when his vison became clear, 'HE WAS MARKED.'

The harsh knock reverberated through the abysmal silence of the palace.

"Who is it?" came Aadrika's voice but there was another knock in reply. She stood up and draped herself in the white silk sheet. The knocking was relentless.

"I am coming."

"She opened the door and was frightened for a moment.

"Yani."

He stood there, his hair out of place, wet from the rain. His clothes stained from travel. Not a single word escaped his mouth as the drops of water on the floor were the only sound and the howling of the wind. Then she noticed the red color.

"What happened to your hand?" she almost screamed. He did not reply. Yani slowly took a few steps and wound his arms around her. The sheet fell on the floor and he rested his head on her bosom. Then she felt the warmth of tears and her eyes saw the missing thumb. The muffled groans reached her ears but not a single word escaped his mouth. She embraced him tightly. Yani buried his head deeper, hiding his face from the world where no one could see.

"It's alright love, it's alright," she whispered. "You are home now, you are safe."

▼

"Are you all right Guruji?"

Sidak opened his eyes. His vision was dim as if he had jumped into a reality where he wasn't supposed to be. He turned around and saw Agni was staring at him along with the others.

"I am fine Param, it's just the sun. I am getting old, am I not?" he said smiling.

"We can rest if you want," said Agni in reply.

"No, that won't be necessary. It was kind of you to ask."

Agni gave a nod and started walking. The others followed suit leaving Sidak standing there. He remained rooted to the spot, a faint smile lingering on his face.

'Another light against the darkness, another sword against the mighty shield. It is not far now.'

"Guruji, guruji," came Param's voice floating to his ears.

Sidak walked in quick steps and found himself standing on a rock overlooking the rippling cascades of water. The smile came back to his face.

"We have found Tiara," beamed Param. Sidak gave a nod. "Yes and there lies Leu," he said pointing where the tall towers reached the sky and the faint outlines could be made even by the naked eye, shrouded in mist yet shining in the Sun.

"Thus it begins."

Epilogue
(The present time, after Agni met Lysandra)

"Hold on boys, we are in for a rough ride. She is nasty today," shouted the Captain of Nirbhay. The waves lashed on the deck and the sails quivered in the wind like leaves. The sky was dark as abyss and the thunder raged like an angry beast.

The sailors scurried around trying to hold the ship together. There was a crackling noise as a bolt of lightning struck the high mast setting it on fire.

"Where is the god forsaken light house of Nisk?" shouted the Captain over the wind.

"I don't see her Captain," shouted back the navigator from the crow's nest.

"Then we are doomed," whispered the Captain more to the wind than his fellow sailors.

The ship jerked horrendously, almost throwing everyone off balance.

"Did we hit something?" shouted the Captain again.

"I don't see anything," came the call of the navigator. The Captain tied the wheel with a rope and rushed towards the other side of the ship. He leaned over the edge as the salt water splashed on his face. Then he heard a scream, a horrible cry which sounded in the sky even in the raging storm. Only to be followed by many more of such.

A sailor soaked in blood of the others came running out on the deck, his eyes wide with fear.

"What is happening down there?" asked the Captain grabbing hold of him.

"There's something below," he cried.

"What is down there, speak man!"

"Red eyes," whispered the sailor in agony over the wind.

"Keep those blades handy and hold her steady till I come up," the Captain shouted the orders. It had been many times that he had seen sailors go mad in the sea but he had to check himself to be certain.

The Captain drew out his blade and started down the stairs leading to general quarters. The lamps swayed with the ship casting shadow and light in awry ways. He took a lamp from the stands. There was blood and gore; one man lay on the floor, with his face down. He rolled him over and gasped taking a step back, the face was ripped off. He looked straight, casting the light from the lamp in his hand on the rest of the place as far as it went. The sight baffled his senses – the sailors were dead, some hung from the ceilings while some were pinned to the wood of the ship. His hand began to shake but he steadied himself. He ran up the flights in frenzy and opened the door to the front deck with a bang.

"Arm yourselves boys, something..." he shouted but the rest of his words trailed off. The men lay dead on the deck, the salt water made the dead bodies sway like rag dolls. The blood stained the wood and the ship rocked with the wind. The navigator fell from the crow's nest and hit the wood with a dull thud.

The sword dropped from his hand. He felt a warm breath on his shoulder and turned around quickly. But he froze with fear. A pair of blood-shot eyes was staring at him, teeth like fangs jutting out of the mouth, the rain lashing on its mammoth form.

The Captain stood there petrified and his feet heavy with dread. Then he felt the taste of blood in his mouth as gurgled out some of it. He looked down and saw the hand of that thing had gone straight through the flesh of his belly.

"Which way is Nisarga?" it asked, a voice as insidious as hell.

The Captain felt his insides twisting and the pain was unbearable, finally his fear gave way to a blood curling scream.

"Which way is Nisarga?"

"North," he almost cried with a blood full of mouth. The monster put his other hand through him and ripped the Captain into two.

Then it gave out a roar, a roar which silenced the storm for a moment and as the thunder raged, the scarred symbol of the chimera on the cracked armour gleamed in the white light.

Death was coming.

About the fictional land of Gaya

The Land of Gaya
The land of Gaya was separated into two large continents –
The Land of the Rising Sun and The Land of the Setting Sun.
There were eight seas and two oceans which surrounded the two
continents. The seas were named after the explorers of the first
era.

The Ages and Eras of Gaya
Gaya had gone through seven ages and the eighth one had started.
The eighth age was then divided by the scholars of the third era
into three eras. The first era started from the rise of Gianna and
ended five hundred years after its downfall, the reasons of which
were still not known. It was said that the men of the west had
travelled east at the end of the first era led by a savior called Vayu
who belonged to the lower caste of the Great Empire of Gianna.
The second era started after that, when the men of the west
settled down again in form of small kingdoms and tribes and the
people of the east flourished as the first city of Chakragarhwas
founded; while the men of the west went south and settled down
at the base of the great mountains. From there, mankind spread
over the entire lands of the east and the west alike. The second
era ended with the founding of great empires in both the shores

of Gaya. The third era began with the founding of the Abode of the Seven in the west and the religion of Trinetra in the east. The third era ended with the prophecy of Darshana and, thus, began the fourth era. Gaya was in the five hundred and twentieth year of the fourth era during the time of Agni.

Languages

The ancient language of Chhanda in the east, also known as the 'Rhyming language' in the west was used during the period of the first era for writing. But there was said to be a general language of which nothing was known by the great gurus or the scholars of the fourth era. The predominant languages which were used in the east were Vakya and Kal; in the west, the language of Dialect was predominant. Other regional languages like Bani, Katha and Akkhar were used in the east; language of the leaf, the murmur of the wind and Bosporas were also predominant in some parts. overall in all, twenty-seven types of languages were used in total by the people of Gaya.

Currency

In the east, Mudra represented gold coins, Gini represented silver coins, and Tama represented copper coins.

$$1 \text{ Mudra} = 24 \text{ Ginis}; 1 \text{ Gini} = 24 \text{ Tamas.}$$

In the west, Bar represented gold, Nuggets represented silver, and Marbles represented copper.

$$1 \text{ Bar} = 30 \text{ nuggets}; 1 \text{ nugget} = 30 \text{ marbles.}$$

Weights and measurements

Weights were measured by iron pellets.

One hand was the length of a standard wooden beam used in every part of Gaya for official measurements.

Sea distances were measured by flights.

1 Flight = 10000 hands.

Land distances were measured by paces.

1 Pace = 10 hands.

But it must be noted that long distances were immeasurable and were counted as per the days generally required to complete the journey.

Time

Time was measured by bell hours by the time keepers: 24 bell hours for one day, 12 for the hours of the Sun and 12 for the hours of the moon, varying with seasons. The sundial was used by the general people to note time and also the bells tolled to inform the coming of a new hour during day time while the time was announced by the time keepers at night.

List of characters

The Land of the Setting Sun –

1. *Aunt Isidora* – The first born of the house of 'Sentinels', elder sister to the fourteenth king of Leu, King Crixus, wife of Lord Hector, the guardian of Hydaspus and the mother of Leo, a member of the southern knights.

2. *Cleon* – Son of Lady Nereus of the noble house of 'Unicorn' of Hydaspus, the captain of the third battalion of the southern knights.

3. *Zoe of Nomantia* – Royal healer of the court of Lord Varca and the childhood friend of Senator Agapito.

The Land of the Rising Sun –

1. *Aranya* – Born to the wife of the local zamindar of the southern villages of Anu, Aranya grew to be a noted scholar under the tutelage of Marut. He was married to Dhara and fathered Charvi.

2. *Charvi* – Daughter of Aranya and Dhara, studying under the mentorship and guardianship of Marut.

3. *Girish, Veer Dasshu* – The famous pirate of the south port of Nada, known to have raided all the villages of the entire coastline of the sea of Jalpath and also to have outmaneuvered the entire fleet of Anu twice. His greatest

victory was raiding the fort of Moru of the desert tribes of Khara from the sea.

4. *Guru Bodhan* — Born in the slums of Viratbhumi, to a family of potters, Bodhan joined the royal army of Raja Vishnu and rose through ranks with his sheer skill of swordsmanship. Later he caught the eye of 'the Pradhan' and was chosen to join 'The Nimit', where he became a guru later on.

5. *Hiranya* — A young Lieutenant of the army of Himadri, rose to the rank of Captain after the death of Paksha. Born to a farmer and his wife in the village of Jaldhar, east of Himadri.

6. *Kalvansh Java* — The prime minister of Brahmadesh and the advisor to Rishi Ketu, their spiritual leader. Java was found by a banyan tree when he was an infant and was brought up under the care of Rishi Ketu himself.

7. *Mahaguru Vajra, Satadru and the Pradhan* — The three torch bearers of the Nimit, the three greater gurus and the highest council of the Land of the Rising Sun led by the Pradhan himself.

8. *Marut* — A noted scholar of Anu, known for his works on the philosophical aspects of craftsmanship and study of ancient runes. Mentor to both Aranya and his daughter, Charvi.

9. *Nikita* — Girish's successor and one of the two children of the famous pirate.

10. *Raja Kabala of Nada* — Born in the village of Kendra, the bastard child of Raja Shambhu of the house of Nath. Kabala was handed over the meager heritage of the small village of Nada for his lowly birth as well as for his relationship to one of the wives of his older brother. Raja Kabala became a pirate and with his wayward ideals and turned Nada into the largest lawless seaport of the east.

*11. **Rishi Bhavesh*** – The spiritual advisor of the king of Anu and one of the five saints to have ascended to the holy land of the southern kingdoms.

*12. **Rishi Ketu*** – The spiritual guardian of Brahmadesh, the protector and leader of her people. He is a descendant of Dhruv and also a brother to Guru Sidak.

The Secrets of the Dark
by Arka Chakrabarti
The Saga of Agni

Is one born with his destiny or does he forge it?

In the mystical land of Gaya, two prophecies bind the fate of men and empires alike. The Destroyer born from the royal seed on the Land of the setting Sun shall bring the empires down, or so has been foretold.

In between the Destroyer and the world stand the Seven Guardians of Gaya, guarding the realm of man. A king, a father, defies the Seven and fate itself to save the last drop of his blood and prince Agni grows in the Land of Rising Sun, exiled from his own people, unaware of his past.

Losing the woman he loved most to the shadows in the dark, Agni is thrown into a whirlpool of events that he neither knows, not understands. His quest for vengeance brings him to the doorstep of a secret that will shatter the very foundation of beliefs of a world.

Can Agni avert his destiny? Can he uncover the truth about the Seven and the prophecies, now hidden behind a veil of ignorance?

The secrets of the dark are sometimes so terrible that they are better left uncovered.